About the Author

A.R Merga is the pen name for Amy Merga and Ryan James. Both have a passion for writing and from a young age they were enthralled by literature, finding themselves drawn into other writers' worlds. What started off as a quick sketch of ideas for a book on a cold winter's night, turned into a full series and a commitment to write. Their dream is to inspire future generations to pick up a book and fall in love, one page at a time, maybe even pen their own.

MAY you FIND Joy
IN READING

The Birt Family Secret and the Tale of Two Worlds

A. R. Merga

The Birt Family Secret and the Tale of Two Worlds

Olympia Publishers
London

www.olympiapublishers.com
OLYMPIA PAPERBACK EDITION

A CIP catalogue record for this title is
available from the British Library.

ISBN: 978-1-78830-708-6

This is a work of fiction.
Names, characters, places and incidents originate from the writer's
imagination. Any resemblance to actual persons, living or dead, is
purely coincidental.

First Published in 2021

Olympia Publishers
Tallis House
2 Tallis Street
London
EC4Y 0AB

Printed in Great Britain

Dedication

To Sandra, Andrea, Aidan, we dedicate this book to you for your support throughout the process of getting it published. To Philip, thank you for always being there to support us and understanding the late nights and early mornings when we disappeared for days on end. Thank you Perry for keeping us sheltered when we needed to get work done. To Kenny, thank you for the incredible artwork which now sits as part of our wonderful book cover. Finally, and perhaps most importantly, thank you to Vida for inspiring us to be the best, your help and support has meant more than you'll ever really know.

Prologue

Charles toppled through the portal backwards, breathing a sigh of relief as it sealed. A plethora of colours shifted to form a twirling rainbow which danced around effortlessly. The motion made a younger Charles vomit. Now he felt numb to the sensation. The wound on his head stung and his vision blurred, yet he fought to stay conscious. On exit, it would be the last chance to speak to his eldest son. The thought of a secure family brought comfort, though the sacrifice meant becoming a casualty in a war no one desired.

Years ago, he elicited an oath to protect all on Earth. The prospect of the Birt's Veil in villainous hands terrified him. He'd have to bequeath it to someone, and on reflection, it had to be his eldest son. Although beat up, it was worth the sacrifice to cut-off those black-eyed kids from his family and Earth. Because of their many forms, it became nearly impossible to track them, searching for years with no luck. Ready to throw in the towel, he located them by chance. A struggle between many meant they were contained in another world. He took solace few sacrificed, so those on Earth could live happily.

The portal burst open and Charles catapulted through the air, crashing into a black and white tiled floor. A piece shattered and punctured his leg. In agony, he propped himself against a cabinet, gasped for air and pulled it out. He pressed a hand over the wound to stem the flow of blood, gathered strength and bellowed two words.

"Victor, kitchen!"

Frightened, he leapt from bed, cursing when he collided with the low-pitched roof. Distressed by his father's voice, he yanked open the bedroom door and sprinted down the staircase. In the kitchen, he flicked on the light, greeted with the sight of his father covered in blood.

"Son, this will be hard to comprehend, but I need you to listen. I can't continue, my time has come."

Victor's face shifted from angry red to pasty white.

"What happened!"

Charles scrunched up his face in concentration.

"They escaped, forced my hand. I did what was right for our family, for everyone."

"Who left no choice, did someone try to rob us? Where are you injured, where'd they go?"

"Not robbed in a physical sense, robbed of time, maybe. I needed more time."

"You've lost too much blood; I should get help."

"Everything's as it should be. You're a reaper, take the Veil, you're next in line."

He lifted his arm to his head and pulled. Victor jumped when a long sleek cloak and a miniscule cane appeared in Charles's hands.

"What the…"

"Listen, I don't have long left!"

"What are those? What do you mean you don't have long left?"

"The Veil of the reaper and the scythe gifted as a weapon of protection. They belong to you."

Victor stepped toward the dining room, debating on calling the paramedics.

"You need first aid!"

"I wanted you to live a human life, like a normal boy. The oldest male of each generation in our family bears the burden and gifts of the Veil."

Victor waited for clarification; none came.

"When I'm gone, head to my study, you'll find two books under the third floorboard. Read them, understand who you are, who you must become!"

He tried to speak, but Charles continued.

"Being keeper of the Veil is crucial. Protect the cycle of life and death and promise me you'll read the books!"

Tears streamed across his face. Their German Shepard Angus moved furtively into the room and flopped beside Charles. Victor called for help, praying somebody could hear, but no one responded. Charles placed a finger over his mouth.

"You're safe, read the books."

"Answer my questions?"

Charles held the scythe.

"Hide this, I ran short of time. Should you need it, someone in our line will locate it."

"I'm calling the paramedics; I have a concussion!"

He raced to the telephone stand in the dining room and clutched the yellow Bakelite phone. It slipped from his clammy hands, but he caught it by the cord and dialled nine - one - one. He dropped the phone as Charles vanished. The black and silver cloak and the small scythe remained. The kitchen tiles looked new, and the blood gone.

He stooped to pick up the items, examining them. Convinced this was a nightmare or the manifestation of a concussion, he turned them. The unexplainable occurred as voices sounded from the corners of the room, words in a language he didn't know formed across the walls and symbols he'd never seen projected upon the roof. The small scythe vibrated, expanding until as tall as Victor and his hand gripped so tight, he couldn't release it.

Whilst preoccupied, the Veil somehow affixed itself. He tried with no luck to remove it. When he peered down, he could see pyjamas, yet in the window, a black and silver cloak wrapped around him. His heartbeat erratically when he glanced at his hands and saw bones. In the reflection, his face had no discernible features. When he looked at his hands again, they were normal. He'd forgotten about Angus until he howled.

A half Rottweiler, half German Shepherd stood, as if spliced. It gnawed at the German Shepherd's side, intent on freeing itself. The Rottweiler appeared as the body separated. It was at least half a size bigger than the Shepherd.

Terrified at what he'd witnessed, he dashed towards the stairs, leaping up them two by two. At the top, he tripped and slid across the floor, his hands catching several splinters. In his parent's room, he cried out, hurling shut the door. Camilla switched on her bedside light and propped herself up.

"Have you had a nightmare; you're covered in sweat?"

"No, I haven't had a nightmare, I might have concussion, but what I've seen is real. I don't know how to tell you, but dad's hurt, and now he's gone!"

"I'm confused, your dad left weeks ago?" said Camilla. "Look what he left."

She passed across a small letter and he read aloud.

'Camilla, this will seem out of the blue, but I feel that

special connection we shared has faded of late. You're my love and the boys my world, but there are myriads of adventure I want to experience. I expect it's hard to understand, but I must leave to forge my own path. One day, it will all make sense. I love you dearly. Yours Always, Charles.'

"I've spoken to him, that's untrue," said Victor, throwing down the letter. "He was downstairs in the kitchen on the floor and pulled this Veil off, now it's stuck to me!"

He pointed to the Veil and tugged the hood. Camilla waved in objection.

"Your brothers handled this with more maturity, and he's four years younger!"

Shocked by the reaction, he broke. Was it a nightmare or concussion?

He pondered how to convince her of the truth. Paws scraped the door, and he opened it, allowing the dog in.

"This isn't Angus. We have a German Shepherd!"

"Go to sleep, you've had a nightmare," said Camilla, getting to her feet. "Enough of this tiresome behaviour!"

"But Mom, I saw with my own eyes, dad told me…"

"Told you what? We've a Rottweiler, your father left weeks ago, and you've had a nightmare!"

Lost for words he pushed through the doorway, passing his brother in the hallway, eavesdropping.

"Dad didn't leave, you believe me, Jimmy?"

"Vicky, dad left weeks ago!"

"Can't you see this Veil, or the scythe in my hand?"

"All I see is pyjamas, idiot! Mom, you sure Vicky isn't adopted?"

He marched into his room, slammed the door and stared in the closet mirror at the Veil, which he hopelessly tugged.

Exhausted, he dropped onto his bed in a rage.

Years passed with bitterness in the household. Camilla struggled, and this drove her mad. Admitted into a mental health institution under twenty-four-hour care, Victor hoped they might release her, but they never did. He tried to keep the family together, but Jimmy had other ideas, leaving for college. Alone in a house, he read the books his father hid. The largest book mentioned the power of the Veil, and a smaller book titled life in the balance explained why reapers exist. The Birt's ancestors agreed to give safe passage to all who deserved it. In return, they received immortality. They agreed to Death's terms, only those ready could move on. This cycle of life and death depended on reapers doing their job. For one to live, one must move on.

He blamed his father for his mother's deterioration, and for the way life turned out, transitioning into the grand reaper making a promise never to have children. He'd never allow someone to go through the emotional trauma he'd suffered. Jimmy met a British exchange student while at college and moved to England. They married and, not long after, started a family. Majoring in architecture, Jimmy's father-in-law showed him one of his favourite buildings, a church in Croston. He studied for a further year, changing careers to become father of that very church. Victor lost touch until he got a letter in the mail some years later. Enclosed was a family photo of Jimmy, his wife and a young baby boy named Michael (Mikey) Birt.

1.

Mikey strutted down the high school corridor to deposit some books in his rather dirty locker. It had been a term since he'd last cleaned it and a curious smell permeated from its vents, a blend of sweaty gym socks and mouldy bread.

Classmates wanted attention, holding out their hands for high fives, congratulating him for scoring the winner in the regional football final.

The Lancashire Boy's trophy arrived home for the first time in decades. The bell sounded and not bothering with religious education; he drifted to the prettiest girl in school.

"Let's skip class and chill on the hill. Who needs religious education!"

She reacted with a series of high-pitched squeals and gripped his hand. He led the way, exchanging glances of elation. Convinced they'd escaped, there was a sharp cough behind them.

"Mr Birt, Miss Beatty, where are you off?"

"Hiya Miss. Taking a shortcut to class, I love religion."

She grimaced when he burst into laughter.

"It's Miss Allen! You find the subject of religion funny, Michael Birt?"

Miss Allen didn't get to point out the rhetorical question.

"No miss, I find it hilarious."

"I beg your pardon!?"

"There's no extraordinary guy in the sky, no one below with a pitchfork, no angels, demons, it's a pile of..."

"A pile of what? In case you've forgotten, you're in a religious school! Head's office now. Tell him why you think the curriculum is laughable. Miss Beatty, don't get dragged down by him, come on, off to class."

She reluctantly surrendered, and he made his way gradually to the Head teacher's office. This time the news would surely reach his father.

"Here to keep me company?"

"Here to see Mr Cawley, Enid. Sorry, Mrs Brown. I debated with Miss Allen."

Mrs Brown smiled against her better judgement.

"Not everyone is open-minded love. I question lots, but remember, we're in a religious school."

In agreement, he slumped into an empty seat. A brief wait later Mr Cawley opened his office door, peered around and covered his face.

"Office, now!"

He dragged his heels through the door, and it slammed shut. Mr Cawley pointed to a tatty red plastic chair.

"This has become a habit, Mr Birt. What have you said this time?"

Mikey held his arm up to speak.

"Ready with your excuse? Let me guess, it wasn't your fault?"

"No sir, could have avoided this if I'd skipped class."

"I suppose it best to avoid argument, what!?"

"I tried to skip class Sir; Miss Allen caught me."

"Did you admit trying to bunk off?"

"Yes sir, no point in religious education."

"Religious education is a fine education; it is staple and paramount to this institution. How dare you try to skip a class; under the law, I could have your parents for this! How would you feel if I were to report you to the local authorities?"

"No need, Sir. I got into a debate with Miss Allen. She erm, misunderstood, and I didn't skip class, did I Sir?"

"That's no excuse for your actions regarding non-attendance of classes. I won't inform the authorities on this occasion, but you lad need to learn a lesson. I think it's high time we got your father involved with this next round of ridiculousness. I wonder what he will think of your escapades. Must be difficult being vicar of our local church and pillar of our community with a troublesome son. Here you are, here you are."

This would be the second time they called his father into school. Last time, a fight broke out with a bully and it took his father to convince the boy's parents not to press charges.

Mr Cawley grabbed the phone, buzzed the receptionist and requested she call Father Birt in.

Half an hour later, he rapped at the office door.

"You may enter."

"Sorry Mr Cawley Sir," said Jimmy, "I was midway through a discussion with a couple about a ceremony. What's he done?"

Mr Cawley tapped his fingers on the desk in contemplation.

"Attempted to skip class, coerce a young female, brought religion into disrepute, offended a religious studies teacher, and acted disrespectfully to a faculty member. Have I missed anything?"

Mikey wriggled on the rickety chair.

"She egged me on! I shared my opinion; she's picking on me!"

"Nonsense, Miss Allen is a model professional, she is a faculty member who does an impeccable job!"

"But Sir!"

Mr Cawley opened his mouth, but the words he looked for came from Jimmy's.

"You're a child, Miss Allen, an adult, respect your elders. She is your teacher, teaching the most important lesson in this school, religion!"

"Well, she…"

"She nothing! Michael Birt, apologise to Mr Cawley for wasting his time, now!"

"Sorry, Sir."

Mr Cawley stood and paced the room. When he didn't speak, Jimmy added.

"I apologise for my son's behaviour; this won't happen again. Michael will be grounded until he differentiates right from wrong. Enough is enough!"

"Thank you. He's great at sport, excellent at English and maths, but has a cheeky streak. We need to iron it out. Perhaps he needs a time out?"

Jimmy grabbed Mikey's collar frog-marching him to the door.

"I agree, he needs time. I'll take him to church, and he'll do repair work for the week. See you at the school service. Good day, Mr Cawley, Sir."

On the drive home, Jimmy lectured on becoming a better person if he followed the word of God. He compared him to his younger twin brothers and how he should act as they do. He'd listened to enough.

"I don't believe in God because the family does, you can't force me. As for the twins, they pretend to behave, you're too stupid to see it!"

"Michael Charley Birt," said Jimmy, punching the steering wheel. "Talk that way again, I'll lock you in your room for a week!"

"But, Dad, listen."

"Enough! I don't want to hear your voice for the rest of the journey. You're grounded until you show the teachers, your mother and God respect!"

Mikey sped across the house, stomping up the stairs into his bedroom. He hurled closed the door, dropping onto his bed in a fit of rage, drifting off to sleep after several frustrated thoughts.

He woke at dawn, disturbed by banging.

"Ooh, your rooms a mess, what's with the hole, dads going to go mental!"

He sleepily glanced to where the twin's voices appeared.

"You knocked a hole through my wall, why!?"

They whispered in tandem.

"Because you'll get in heaps of trouble and it makes our day, ha-ha!"

"You won't get away with this!"

Mikey cursed, and both parents rushed upstairs barging in.

"What's the noise about?"

"Lo-look what he did to our w-w-wall Dad! He punched straight through. It scared the poo out of us!"

"That hole will cost you! I've had enough of your antics, Mister!"

The twins looked at the floor, weeping behind their hands.

When Jimmy looked away, they smirked, then carried on the charade.

"This family is dysfunctional," said Mikey, shaking with anger. "Apparently the sun shines out the twin's bottoms, and I'm a constant disappointment!"

"You ungrateful, spoiled brat. Do you know what dysfunctional means!?"

"Dysfunctional is this family, you're full of yourself. You run a church in a small village, for Christ's sake!"

"That hole is one step too far! Pack your bags, go live with your uncle for a while. You'll soon appreciate how together we have it!"

"Fine! Be an improvement to here. I've never met the bloke, but he's better than you!"

He clutched a suitcase cramming clothes in, forced the zips closed and snatched up his wallet and passport.

"How am I getting to uncle Victor's, broomstick!?"

"You can stay in this room until you apologise!"

"Never going to happen!"

"Enough, you stay here. You two, go downstairs. I hope B&Q have plasterboard to fix this mess!"

The twins scuttled from the room, keen to please their father.

"I mean it, you stay until you apologise, Mister. I will bring lunch up. No TV, phone or games console!"

When the bedroom door closed, he switched on his laptop and searched for flights. He used his savings card to purchase a ticket and printed them off. Sick to death of the threats, he snatched the tickets and stormed downstairs.

Jimmy appeared at the front door where he stood.

"I ordered you to stay in your room?"

"You insisted I live with Victor. If I'm not wanted, drop me to the airport and I'll be out of your hair!"

"Accept you're wrong and apologise!"

"For being the only witness to the twin's charades? They put that hole in the wall, not me!"

"Liar, you're out of control. I suggest you march upstairs!"

"I'm done with you and those idiot brothers; I want to live with Victor!"

"You want to live with your uncle? You have one last chance to apologise for your behaviour!"

He waved an A4 piece of paper in front of him.

"Yeah, I paid for a ticket with the money I'd saved. You know the money I earn, since I get nothing. I won't live somewhere I'm not wanted."

"This what you want, Mister? To settle with your dislodged uncle, above your family?"

"It'll be better than this hellhole!"

Jimmy grabbed his car keys and looked to his wife.

"If he can buy a ticket, he's old enough to go to his uncle's. I'll call Victor on the way. Don't look at me like that. He made this decision; he's going, and that's final!"

The door slammed closed and the unmistakable roar of the twins' laughter spread through the house. On the drive to the airport, Jimmy didn't speak or acknowledge him. Once outside the terminal he pulled the handbrake and turned off the engine.

"You still want to do this? You walk through those doors, and you don't come back until you apologise to your brothers, your teachers and me!"

"You'd love that, back with my tail between my legs! I hate you and that family, bye!"

He snatched the suitcase from the boot of the car, pulled the handle and rolled it along to the entrance doors, not glancing back. Once he checked the bag, he passed through security at a snail's pace, looking up from his phone when a voice yelled.

"Sir, yes you with the mobile! Put your personal artefacts, belts, shoes etc in these trays, then step through the scanner!"

He followed the instructions, and the alarm blared. Surrounded by three security personnel, he searched around.

"Do you have any piercings, sharp objects, batteries, lighters, or any other items in your possession?"

"No, I have nothing, or any piercings."

One of them searched his belt line and then used a mobile metal detector to sweep his body and it went off near his pocket. He instinctively put his hand near it.

"Please don't do that, sir! Keep your hands by your sides!"

He placed his hand in Mikey's pocket, turning it inside out. A five pence piece rolled off under the bag scanner. They did another sweep and cleared him to pick up his things. Why did Airports always make everyone feel guilty?

2.

Arriving at JFK after a two-hour delay, he filtered with the crowd towards the exit to meet his uncle, where groups loitered the atrium. Some carried cardboard with names, some had plastic boards, and a few VIP chauffeurs held LED displays embossed with their client's names. Unable to see his own, he waited at the terminal exit, using his suitcase as a seat. When Victor didn't show, he headed to the roadside to flag down a yellow cab, threw his case into the boot and sat in the back. The driver turned as the door closed.

"Where to kid?"

"Can I please go to Milford, Connecticut," he said, eyeing a scribbled note. "I think the post code or zip code, is zero six four six zero."

"Kid, Milford's quite a way, it'll cost you. You got the cash?"

"How much?"

"About a hundred bucks. It's an hour and a half away and there're tolls to pay."

"I have a hundred, thank you."

The driver set off, stopping now and again to allow pedestrians to cross to various car parks.

"If you don't mind me asking, why's a kid at the airport on his own, where's your parents?"

The driver eyeballed him through the rear-view mirror.

"Long story short, I'm here to live with my uncle after I fell out with my dad and he threatened me. I called him out on his bluff and here I am."

"We've all been there, parents don't understand kids, we don't understand them, it's a generational thing. By the time you're my age with your own family, you'll understand."

He nodded out of courtesy.

"Why didn't this uncle collect you from the airport?"

"Not sure. My dad called him before I left."

The driver shrugged.

"Sounds like one hell of a family. What's your name?"

"Michael, but my friends call me Mikey."

"I'm Tony, Tony Romero. Where you from, I don't recognise the accent?"

The driver sensed his nervousness, making the journey easier.

"I'm from Lancashire, my mum's English and dad's American. I lived about an hour from Liverpool."

"I love Liverpool, two of the best soccer teams out there! Are you a red or a blue?"

"I don't support any, against the best wishes of my mum, who supports the blue side."

"Who do you follow? You like soccer?"

"I support Bolton. You don't pick the team, they pick you."

"Fair enough. I'll show you some sights along the way. We pass over some famous bridges and if the weather's clear, you'll see the outline of Manhattan, and other famous landmarks, it's part of the service!"

Tony followed through on his word, pointing out several sights. He pulled over so Mikey could take pictures of the

Manhattan skyline, his dream place to visit. They moved on, discussing subjects youths shared no interest in. He ranted, swerving between several lanes of traffic when he lost Mikey's interest.

"Kids today with technology. You don't live in the real world, communicating through cell phones and computers, come on!"

Sensing Tony's gaze in the rear-view mirror, he placed his phone away, pointing to a sign as they crossed over an old iron drawbridge.

"Devon, we have a county back home named the same."

"England populated America, kid. It's understandable some names stuck. You're in New England. Okay, this is Spring street, how far down is the house?"

"About halfway, it's white with a big front yard and driveway."

"All the houses on this street are similar, any unique features?"

"It's got a porch, and the fence is a chain-link one at the front, wood at the sides."

"I see it ten houses up. You sure it's the right place, it looks condemned?"

"Yeah, it's my uncle's house, inherited from his father."

"I'm not comfortable dropping you here. Maybe I should wait until your uncle comes out. Can you call him on your cell phone?"

"I've not got an American sim card. I can visit his car yard if he's not here. Thank you for bringing me!"

"Call it fifty bucks, then you got money for yourself."

"Thanks Mr, I appreciate it."

"You find yourself in need of a tour guide near Manhattan,

look Tony up. Take care, kid."

He handed over a card and drove down the street slowly.

With the cab gone, he took in the house his father's side grew up in, unable to process its dilapidated state. The weeds in the front yard stood higher than the fence, and ornamental grass sprouted out of control like hair from an old man's ears. At the flaking front door, he shifted a spider making its way up his arm. Careful not to harm it, he placed it on the fence, watching it scatter. A whiff of peeled paint and damp wood filled the air. The wood clad walls seemed rotten, the opposite to photographs of the house in its heyday. Afraid the rusted doorknob would crumble; he twisted it and pressed his shoulder against the door. The frame groaned and dropped. Searching for other entrances, he broadcast his uncle's name now and then.

The backyard had more shrubs than you could shake a stick at. Faced with another locked door, he booted a stone flowerpot and it rolled down the yard. He regretted it as an intense pain shot through his foot. Eyeing a rock intent on breaking a window, an object caught his attention on the flagged floor. The anger subdued when he spotted a big brass door key underneath a small amount of dirt.

The rusted lock protested as the key turned and when it released, he shoved against the door and it flew open. Old paint and woodchips scattered, and after swotting several sticky webs, he entered the kitchen. A once pristine room stood lost with a layer of dust an inch thick. It was obvious the room wasn't used. At a closed door on the upper level, he knocked.

"Uncle Victor, you in there?"

A few seconds passed, and he opened the door. Met with the smell of musty bed sheets and damp, he scrunched his nose in disgust. Worried the floorboards might collapse, he stepped around a rotten one and stopped near an old chest of drawers to rifle through. At the creak of floorboards, he twisted to see a Rottweiler round the doorway. It snarled, baring its teeth, ready to strike at any moment.

"Good boy, it's okay, shush, friendly dog. Oh God, please don't eat me!"

He made himself as tiny as possible, backing into a corner. A sound like the crack of a whip startled him.

"Angus, No! You there, how bloody dare you peruse my private quarters! I instructed you to leave my house alone. Get out, or I'll call the cops!"

"Uncle Victor, it's me, Mikey."

Victor grabbed a photo from the pouch in his wallet and surveyed it. A long silence passed, then he broke into laughter.

"Finally, we meet! You're six feet taller than in the picture I have. How time flies!"

Victor's smile vanished, and he turned defensive.

"If you're here, then your father is too. He gets no money, not one cent! He, he abandoned us!"

Terrified of the dog backing him into the corner, he choked.

"Make him stop?"

"Don't worry," said Victor rolling his hand lazily through the air, "He's all bark. Leave Mikey alone!"

Angus backed off reluctantly, looking disappointed. Tall and dressed in black, Victor had dark brown hair with streaks of grey tied up into a ponytail sat lazily over his shoulder. He looked a taller, slimmer version of his father. No longer pinned in the corner, Mikey tried to stand and stumbled. Victor pulled him up into a bear hug.

27

"Come here! You look like an athletic, happier version of me. Hope your old man didn't draw the fun out of you?"

Startled by affection, he froze.

"I assume your father is around. How was the flight? Not to turbulent, I hope?"

"The flight was okay, delayed by a few hours. I wondered why you weren't at the airport?"

"I didn't know you were coming?"

"My dad left you messages, I thought I heard him talk to you?"

Victor glanced to the unhooked phone in the corner.

"Got no messages, are you sure he called me, and not his wife's brother? Where's your old man?"

"He's, at home. He sent me to live with you, said I was trouble and needed to learn what dysfunctional meant."

"Absolutely not, you can't stay! This isn't a suitable home for a young man, I am no guardian!"

Victor investigated the dusty dressing-table mirror.

"As for dysfunctional, I prefer the term slightly unhinged."

"I'm not going back. They made life hell. I'd rather be on the streets, plus I only bought a one-way ticket!"

"You purchased your own ticket?"

"Yeah, they never give me anything but grief and hand-me-downs, I'm the bad sheep of the family."

"You mean the black sheep?"

"You can't say that, it's politically incorrect."

"It's a saying, it won't hurt anyone, calm down. Forgive me, I'm a little out of touch with society."

"I agree, the nineteen eighties called; they want their clothes back!"

"Why, you cheeky little... perhaps I was hasty. I think we'll get along fine. I don't have any rules, other than stay out my business, keep your nose clean and have a bloody shower because you my boy stink!"

A tremendous weight lifted from Mikey's shoulders.

"I'm looking for normality. That said, what happened to the house?"

Victor shifted his weight, uncomfortable with the question.

"We agreed you'd stay out of business. You seem tired, get off to bed, you've had a long flight. Use the guest room at the bottom of the corridor, it's the cleanest, used to be my haunt! Off with you, chop, chop!"

Victor ushered him from the room. Too tired to argue, he walked to the guestroom opening the door.

The bedroom had new linen, curtains and fresh crisp wallpaper. Mikey sure he'd seen the room a mess, put it down to tiredness, undressed, and collapsed onto the bed. How great it would be to wake, undisturbed by his devious brothers.

3.

He woke to hushed voices outside the bedroom. The door opened, revealing the silhouette of an elderly man. A hand floated over his shoulder, pulling him backwards.

"Quiet," said Victor, "he's not an animal in a zoo to obsess over. Now grab a brush!"

"I hoped to glimpse the idiot daft enough to live under the same roof as you!"

"Unless you fancy early retirement, be quiet, old man!"

"You wouldn't dare attempt anything, you need me."

"If you wake him, I'll risk it! Close the door!"

Furniture scraped floors, pots and pans clattered, and various noises echoed through the hallway. Eventually they died down and he tossed and turned, unable to sleep. Now and again he sensed someone stop short of the room to listen. A floorboard creaked, and a shadow blocked the light that filtered through the gap in the door, confirming his suspicions. Angus took long, heavy breaths and sniffed the air. The rest of the night he lay awake, paranoid. Why had the dog taken an interest?

Daylight crept through the lazily drawn curtains and unable to get back to sleep, he started the day early. When the door opened, the scurry of paws across wood made him peer out. He caught the rear end of Angus shuffling down the stairs.

The floors were spotless; the walls painted with no trace

of fumes, and the cracked ceiling and walls repaired twelve hours after he'd seen the house a mess. The distinct sound of a vinyl record scratched and bumped until Victor changed it, singing along to Sinatra.

"Morning pal," said Victor, "hope I didn't wake you? It's impossible to sleep, not that I have a choice. Breakfast?"

He nodded, taking a seat.

"You cleaned, painted, and repaired an entire house overnight?"

"I had a helping hand, don't worry. You've got a busy day; you need a school uniform for Milford academy. I'll hand you cash, get what you need, treat yourself to take out in town."

"You registered me into a school, overnight?"

"I called in a favour."

"Did you call the president?"

"We agreed you'd stay out of my business?"

"An academy? Can't I attend a normal school, with no uniform, like in TV shows?"

"The school is a fine institution with an outstanding record of education. Your father and I attended!"

"That's what worries me."

"What was that?"

An argument with someone he'd moved in with wasn't the best way to start a relationship. Suspicious, he took the money handed over.

"Who were you chatting with last night?"

"Angus, perhaps?"

"The bedroom door opened, and I caught the figure of a tiny man?"

"Ha-ha, that sounds like a wicked dream. Long flights can do that to you, scary thing jet lag."

"Angus came to the door, sniffing underneath. I didn't sleep well; he's got it in for me."

"Definitely a dream buddy. He was with me this morning!"

"I watched his fat bum shuffle downstairs?"

Victor shrugged. He looked thin and pale for a man of six feet seven inches.

"You ok, you look ill?"

"I'm fine. Had enough cereal? I've business to attend too, so when you're ready, away you go!"

Mikey pushed the chair backwards and collected his coat and wallet. After a wrong turn down a side street, he located the bus stop and hailed one down. The driver slammed on the brakes and the skid of tyres brought it to a halt. He paid for his ticket, taking a seat next to an elderly lady, dressed in an oversized parker coat.

At the station, he followed signs for the town centre, a ten-minute stroll away. Peckish, he visited a sandwich store and purchased a foot-long sub, a real meaty treat smothered in copious amounts of ketchup. Breakfast comprised stale cereal, which he hadn't fancied as the malt balls were like mini boulders and would destroy his teeth!

The various businesses dotted about were impressive, from a historic sweet shop to a girly fashion store and one that caught his eye, a games store crammed full of goodies. The town provided shops for every hobby. He gazed into the window at the latest console, forgetting about the uniform. On the bus, he remembered and rushed back, peeved over his forgetfulness. He skirted several groups, dumbfounded by rudeness when none attempted to go single file. He barged through a couple and they hurled abuse. Intent on responding, he collided with someone. The clatter of scattered books and stationery forced him to stop. A girl around his age scowled from the floor, and he offered his hand.

"I was rushing to the uniform shop."

Her cheeks blushed, she seemed utterly furious.

"You knocked me over, moron!"

She collected her items and grabbed his hand, pulling herself up.

"Thanks, Robo cop. Pay attention in future!"

"I didn't see you. A rude couple annoyed me."

"Two wrongs don't make a right?"

"Sorry?"

The girl brushed her hair to the side.

"The uniform shop closes in thirty minutes."

"They do uniform for the posh school?"

"Ugh, yeah," said the girl. "That's my school, unfortunately."

"Is it that horrible?"

"You'll see. I need to buy a new tie, mine's worn, don't think I'm stalking you!"

He laughed as they set off in the same direction together. Half an hour later, they stepped outside, and he insisted on helping her carry the bags once she calmed down. They had loads in common and keen to continue the conversation. He invited her to a diner across the street.

"Let me buy you some pop, soda, as a way of apology?"

"Pop," said the girl with a smile. "What's your name, I can't call you the clumsy boy who knocked me flying forever?"

"Mikey, Mikey Birt."

"Well Mikey, Mikey Birt, I'm Eva, Eva Lyfer. Welcome

to the wonderful hole named Milford!"

As they crossed the sidewalk, he took in the town. It looked wonderful, far from the hole she referred to. He held the door, and she mumbled about being able to open it herself. They entered awaiting a server. An old-looking waitress wandered over.

"Table for two dears?"

At a booth with green leather seats, they sat taking two menus from the waitress who collected used plates to return to the kitchen. The variety of items astounded him, each one laden with sufficient calories to fire a rocket to the moon. The pictures of pancakes, griddles, and many other unhealthy dishes made his belly rumble. After a few minutes, the waitress returned.

"What'll it be kids?"

"I'll order," said Eva impatiently. "We'll take two chocolate shakes and two twisted fries, please."

"Is that everything?"

"Yeah, thank you."

The waitress collected the menus, headed to the kitchen to place the order.

"That's not fair, you've been here longer. You probably don't get caught up in the menus, there's a huge choice!"

"Women know what they want, men take forever to decide!"

"There's three thousand items on this menu, I want to try them all. I'll do them in my order!"

"Yeah, Yeah."

"How long you lived here?"

"This time?"

"You've settled here more than once?"

"When I was younger, my parents wanted a fresh start, so we emigrated. They fell out, and we moved back to Australia. It didn't work out, so we ended up in Stratford. Been here six years and counting."

"You live with your parents?"

"With my mum," said Eva, thumping the table. "My dad ran away with a dental nurse half my mum's age. We have dual citizenship, so moved back without the git!"

"I don't mean to be nosy; I want to get to know you."

"What about you, a Scottish kid in America? What's your story?"

"I'm not Scottish, I'm English. From a village near Liverpool."

"Your accent's peculiar compared to any English accent I've heard. The one I understand is the Queen's English, darling!"

"Not everyone speaks like the Queen, we've hundreds of dialects in the UK."

The conversation took a back seat when the waitress delivered their order. He slurped at the thick chocolatey shake and clutched a fistful of fries, loading them into his mouth.

"What's this school like?"

"All right, unless you're from out of town, they stick to their own."

"Don't worry, at my last school, I had them eating out my hand!"

"You're a get popular type, they'll eat you alive. It's late, I should head home!"

Sensing he'd caused offence, he offered to walk her home. In front of the house, an awkward attempt to ask for her cell phone number ended up a mishmash of jumbled words. This was fresh territory.

"Eva, can I have a number, I mean can I have your number?"

She blushed a crimson colour.

"Yeah, but you'll forget about me, I blend into furniture."

She scrolled through her handset, and he copied her number.

"Thanks for walking me home."

He awkwardly curtsied and wandered away. On the way home, he opted for a shortcut through a park. Halfway across a field, a strange echoing noise sent chills up his back. A fierce wind blew dust, and he rubbed his eyes. When it subsided, he uncovered them and for a second, swore he spotted someone in the distance. Not taking any risk at night in a poorly lit park, he backtracked. It would be longer, but the safer option.

No one was home. His uncle had taken Angus, thank goodness! Passing time, he explored the house properly. Pulling a draw chord, the loft hatch descended to reveal an unsteady wooden ladder. Dust made him cough and splutter as he ascended.

At the top he fumbled for a light switch, pulling a cord which bathed the enormous loft in light. It stretched the length of the house.

Halfway, he found several boxes with labels like 'Family photos, vacations, etc.' He browsed through them and paused at one of his fathers. How did he go from jack the lad to grumpy Vicar? He browsed glimpsing a photo of two older people. The back of the photo had four words written neatly in faded black ink, 'Charles and Camilla Birt'. Though he'd never met them, he knew they were his grandparents.

His uncle looked like Charles, who was tall and thin.

Mikey remembered when his dad said Victor was the brat, but the pictures pointed to Jimmy being the spoilt one. In every picture he sported new toys, while Victor held shabby hand-me-downs. Mikey and his uncle had the same experience growing up.

Full of dust, he showered to clear the swirl of thoughts that roamed around. Still not home. He assumed his uncle worked late. He sought entertainment, making his way to the lounge room in search of a TV. When he couldn't locate one, he opted for an early night to catch up on sleep. He'd call Eva in the morning to see if she wanted to meet.

A voice disturbed him, and he crept outside to listen, hanging over the handrails.

"Angus, we must remain calm. My father was an odd character, but not short sighted. He would've mentioned this, though I don't recall it!"

He caught a view of his uncle, and Angus sat on the sofa. He couldn't believe how affectionate he was until Victor held out his hand to pass over some chicken!

"For years, they seemed calm and content to live where they were, now they cause trouble for surrounding folk. Why the sudden change, what are they planning?"

Angus appeared to shake his head in response.

"You won't know, it's not your job. I think he warned us, well, me about this. Why are they restless?"

Unable to make heads or tails of the conversation, Mikey crawled to bed.

4.

He watched a couple of songbirds playing through his window. One seized a worm from another's beak, lost its balance and dropped from the oak tree, taking flight before reaching the ground. It landed on the branch, rustling its feathers. With no true nature spots, minus a few parks, it surprised him how they adapted to urbanisation considering back home birds were everywhere, especially in the woodlands surrounding the village. Met with the delightful scent of bacon and pancakes from downstairs, he grasped the handrail and glided down, stopping at the foot of the stairwell. Victor didn't notice him wander into the kitchen and hummed away, flipping a pancake with remarkable precision until he caught Mikey's reflection in the window and nearly dropped the pan.

"Pancakes! I made fluffy tasty treats for my favourite nephew, with the finest crispy bacon and real maple syrup, not the artificial kind you pick up at fast-food joints!"

"You sound like a cheesy advertisement from cable TV, where's the camera hidden?"

"A nutritionally balanced breakfast is crucial to starting the day."

"Pancakes, nutritious, yeah sure, I believe you."

He loaded a stack onto a plate and handed them across, winking as he did. Mikey took a knife and fork, stuffing a piece into his mouth, and the complexity of the flavours on his palate blew him away with every bite. Unable to communicate, he nodded towards his uncle in thanks and scoffed more.

"You'd think it the last supper, no pun intended," said Victor. "Not a jab at your old man, honest!"

Mikey covered his mouth to stop rogue pieces of pancake escaping. Finishing a glass of squeezed orange juice, he grabbed the plates and took them to the sink, but Victor interrupted.

"I'll sort the dishes; I find it therapeutic. Onto important matters, I've got you a gift, I'm told it is what youths crave. Follow me into the lounge."

Mikey's jaw dropped as he glanced at the fifty-inch, eight K, high definition television and underneath lay the latest games console on the market.

"No way, you entered the twenty-first century, this equipment costs a fortune, did you re-mortgage the house!?"

"Silly boy. I see I made the right decision as it seems people still watch television for entertainment. I hear youths of today play these game stations. I thought I'd let you join the masses, that's what Father advised."

"Father? What are you on about?"

"The store I purchased the equipment from is family-owned. The father supported his son with the sale."

With no reason to ask questions, Mikey thanked him and shifted his attention to the television and games console. He switched it on, flicking through the channels.

"I did a grocery shop as my job keeps me in the office and I have a consignment of automobiles to accept. Occupy yourself as you wish. Cars won't trade themselves!"

"I'll pop over later and lend a hand. May as well join the family business?"

Victor rubbed his head.

"Thank you, but it's not a place for a young man, it's a serious business."

"I've obsessed over cars forever. Besides, you must have muscle cars, I don't mind honest, I'm decent with a spanner!"

Victor's face reddened, and he turned defensive.

"I don't require help from a snotty-nosed teenager. If I needed help, I would ask an adult. Now go play your game station thing, I've got work to complete. See you later!"

Victor left with Angus in tow and closed the door behind him.

He shrugged off his uncle's outburst, focusing his attention on the console. Its sleek design features and its technical specification made the latest Gamestation something to behold.

An hour passed, and he glanced at his watch. Avoiding thoughts about school, the nerves kicked in as he got ready and it dawned, he would be the new kid. Maybe it wouldn't be a walk in the park.

He called Eva to see what she was doing.

"Hello, Mikey, how's it hanging?"

"Hi Eva, I'm trying to phone my uncle, got confused by all these numbers. While I have you, fancy hanging out before school?"

"I suppose I can be persuaded to find the time."

"You suppose, cheers!"

"You mentioned you called me by accident, just getting you back."

"Fair play, I deserved that, I guess."

"There's a park near school, meet you at the entrance in an hour?"

"Magic, look forward to it, see you then."

They met forty minutes before lessons started outside the gates. He fumbled with his tie, something he'd never got the hang of doing up. Sometimes being left-handed was a curse.

"I can't believe you can't do a tie up at sixteen. Did your mummy do it for you?"

"I can too! I take care of myself thanks, have done since eleven years old."

"Come here, it's not rocket-science, Einstein!"

She explained a five-step process of how to do a tie, and he pretended to listen. They strolled to school, taking in the scenery of the oldest park in town. The pathways were strewn with leaves from trees as tall as four-storey buildings.

Skimming around the edge of a glimmering lake, a strange sensation in the pit of his stomach took hold. Eva sensed his emotional struggle.

"Don't worry, you're the popular kid; it'll be a walk in the park, remember?"

Stepping through the gates, the main high school with its brown brick walls came into view. He wondered if they'd converted a prison. It appeared more prison than place of education.

"Follow the corridor to the end of the hall. Turn right at the bottom and Reception will help you. Message me later?"

She left, and he headed down the large corridor, stopping to glance at a cabinet full of American football trophies. The school had many accolades.

The clinical walls had pictures of famous students. An erected picture showed a magician with a Saturday night show on television. He glimpsed part of it this morning and thought it seemed awful, making him question how outstanding this school was.

With masses of paperwork filled, he attempted to get the receptionist's attention. She chatted on the phone, oblivious to the world. He tried not to listen and coughed to get her attention. She stared through narrowed eyes, bid farewell to the person on the line, and snatched his paperwork. With a map and timetable, he headed to his form room in the maths department.

He entered the maths block, searching until he found a plaque on a door that read.

'Room Ten, Mr George Watford.'

He knocked, making out students and a teacher through the frosted window.

"You may enter."

He twisted the doorknob, and it slipped from his grip. He wiped his hands on his pants and tried again. The door opened, and the class fell silent, turning to look at him.

"Ah, you must be Michael? I'm Mr Watford. Grab a seat, make yourself at home. I'm sure everyone here will help you feel welcome, right guys?"

The class responded with the generic 'yes sir'.

He grabbed a seat at the front, hoping to blend into the furniture.

Mr Watford completed the register and walked to Mikey, picking up the form on the desk.

"Now registrations complete, can we please welcome Michael Charley Birt? I see you come from England, a fellow Brit! What brings you to the grand old USA?"

When he didn't reply he continued.

"I see you were soccer captain, to us brits, football!"

The class jeered, and Mr Watford put his hand up.

"Quiet! Michael, this is your form, relax, students here are great, though America take's it's sports seriously."

A bell sounded throughout school, signalling the start of classes. The first lesson would be English.

Students shoved chairs back, and they moved towards the exit. The squeak of rubber soles on the corridor floor filtered out as they left. Before he vacated, Mr Watford spoke.

"Kids here are cruel, they don't handle new people. Keep your head screwed on. Any problems, see me."

"Okay, Sir. Thanks."

He pulled open the door, took one nervous glance at the teacher, then walked through the corridor to English.

This teacher had the worst breath imaginable. Worse still, he kept leaning over Mikey's desk to instruct the class. When the bell rang signalling the first break of the day, he waited till everyone left, then took out his phone to text Eva.

A response came through a minute later, informing him she was in the library. He found her and she signalled over to the research section, pointing to a seat.

"I sense an unhappy Mikey today; this school's weird, isn't it?"

"People stare and whisper like naughty nursery children in the playground."

"A nursery, isn't that where they raise plants from seedlings?"

"No, not that type, I think Americans call it preschool, or something like that?"

She leant against the desk with both elbows, propping her head up.

"We both have chemistry last period. Want to walk me home? I should study, but we can hang out, do it together?"

"Yeah, we can swing by my uncle's car yard on the way. Only seen it in photographs, he's dead protective."

"I never asked about you, do you live with your uncle? What happened to your parents?"

Impressed Eva asked two questions in quick succession, Mikey answered through gritted teeth.

"My parents think I'm a disappointment and my dad bluffed me, so I called him out. He sent me with my uncle to learn what the word dysfunctional meant. They didn't expect me to prefer it here, or to buy the ticket myself!"

"Correct me if I'm wrong, but in England you go to school until sixteen? That means you need to add another two years to your education!"

"Another two years, you're joking, I was in my last year at St Michaels!"

"Everyone knows in America you attend until you're eighteen."

"Not fair! I thought I'd finish this year and help my uncle at his car yard."

"You're stuck at Milford Academy till eighteen, you can't empty a bin without a qualification in this state!"

The bell rang for the start of next class and they parted ways. Attending school until eighteen made him feel annoyed and relieved at the same time. His friends back home had goals and plans, but he didn't. Last class arrived, Mikey's second least favourite subject, chemistry.

Students queued along the corridor, messing around while away from adult supervision. One boy fabricated paper darts and flung them at people with a thick yellow elastic band. Eva dodged one and stuck her finger up. Mikey grabbed her shoulder, and she defended herself.

"Get off, oh, it's you. Feeling any better? I was thinking a few showrooms and garages around town sell cars? Tell me the name and we'll head there after class."

"Remind me not to annoy you, temper, temper! My uncle's place is Brum Motors, the biggest car lot in town."

"They shut Brum Motors years ago. My mum bought a car from there, a total lemon. The guy who owned it seemed proper creepy; don't know what happened."

"It's been in my family for sixty years. My grandad owned it before my uncle, may go back further."

"There may be another around town, but the one I visited closed after I arrived in Connecticut the second time."

"It can't be closed. He leaves the house before I'm up most days and arrives back late at night. He stops out occasionally as he picks up cars from out of town."

"Unless he opened another place? All I know is there's one Brum Motors, and it's been derelict for years."

He brushed off the information, convinced it was another place, and tried to change the conversation. The bell rang and out came the science teacher to usher them in.

Grateful the first day concluded, they made their way through the grounds, walking down the main street to a side road where his uncle's car yard should've been. Full of trees, shrubs and broken signage, as Eva said, the lot lay abandoned. Strewn over the crumbled asphalt were various bits of glass from old window panels, vandals smashed. The concrete supports for the fences crumbled away and the only vehicle remaining, a rusted pickup truck, had an old advertisement board on top. Its tyres were rotten and green algae and moss protruded from them. He hoped there were two Brum Motors in town, suggesting they find the other. She pointed to a gatepost with a plaque.

"151 Lexington Avenue, Proprietors C. Birt and Sons Motors, trading as Brum Motors. Looks like this is your uncle's place. It's been closed for years."

He kicked a lamp post, hurting his foot.

"This is where my uncle goes! Why would he lie to me, it makes no sense?"

She grabbed his hand, pulling him into a hug. He forgot the confusion and upset for a moment.

'Maybe there's a valid reason he didn't tell you. He's probably embarrassed to admit the family business has gone under. If it was me, I wouldn't mention it.'

"You're right, I'll bring it up, see what he has to say when I get home later."

Eva walked him home to make sure he was ok. They stopped by a twenty-four-hour convenience store to purchase a drink. At the house, she gawped.

"This is where you live? We avoid it at Halloween and Christmas. Rumour is, it's haunted by a deranged spirit which escaped from a local mental ward."

"The only thing haunting this house is my uncle's scary dog, Angus!"

When he offered her a tour, she accepted? Amused how nosy Eva was, he wondered if she'd even seen a house before. She searched every cupboard, drawer, nook and cranny, like a toddler would.

"You're so nosy, have you ever been in a house before?"

She poked her head from a cupboard, slapping him playfully on his arm.

"Cheeky. I'm fascinated by how a house can seem derelict and at risk of collapse, then days later, sparkle like a show home? I've peeked through the windows before. It was filthy."

"Apparently miracles happen but I still can't explain it, went right over my head!"

"Overnight? come on, that's impossible, who helped him, an army of tradespeople?"

"I fell asleep in a house full of dust, woke up in a brand new one."

"He would need builders, plumbers, electricians and cleaners to get it up to shape?"

"I don't know, blew my mind to be honest when I stepped out in the morning to a clean house and my uncle's creepy mutt. Want some soda?"

"I love root-beer, try it with ice cream, root-beer floats are delicious!"

"Ice cream in a fizzy drink, that sounds awful, no offence. That's like putting milk with Vimto or peanut butter with jam."

"I love peanut butter and jelly. Is Vimto an English thing?"

"Only the single best soft drink ever created. A purple fruity drink that can be consumed hot or cold, sold in many countries around the world, like England, Saudi Arabia, etc."

He poured a drink as Victor arrived home. He strolled into the kitchen with Angus trotting behind.

"Fancy Chinese tonight, I feel we deserve a film night, let our hair down so to speak. Wait, you girl, get out this house, your kind isn't welcome! Leave now!"

She ran to the door, terrified. Mikey gave chase but couldn't keep up as she sprinted down the steps and out the front gate.

"Eva, wait, my uncle can be crazy, he didn't mean it. Come back!"

He marched inside the house, slamming the door,

absolutely livid.

"What the hell? She's my friend. Why're you acting like a psychopath!?"

Victor looked furious. He punched a wall several times, and a picture crashed to the floor, its frame smashing to pieces.

"I forbid you to see that girl. You have broken a house rule, one I clearly told you about. Don't ask me questions, do as I say!"

"You said there were no rules. You can't act like that, she's a guest, and that's not how you treat them!"

"Did I invite her into my home? You seek permission to have guests in my house at all times!"

"I get it, I'm a guest. Looks like you and my father have tonnes in common. You don't act like that towards a girl, ever!"

"Do as you're told. I'm away tonight, I suggest you go to your room and remain there, do you understand?"

"You discuss food, glance at Eva, flip out, and now you're out for the night, I don't get it?"

"I need time to process what happened. This isn't black and white!"

"What happened? She's a girl, you know, a female, like your mum, or my mum, not some alien species?"

"Don't you ever, under any circumstances, talk about my mother, you know nothing about her!"

Victor's eyes became bloodshot and a vein at the side of his temple throbbed so much it looked fit to burst.

"What's your problem, seriously, are you sure you're feeling alright upstairs, you know, in the head?!"

Victor slumped to the floor clutching his chest, and Angus growled, staring at Mikey through narrowed eyes.

"I don't have a problem in the slightest. I'm staying with a friend tonight. No more questions if you please!"

"I'm sorry I mentioned your mum, well grandma, but you have no excuse for the way you acted, and this isn't over by any means. I expect you to apologise to Eva when you get back from your little adventure!"

"Go to your room, before Angus escorts you and stands guard for a week!"

He ran upstairs, slammed the bedroom door and used his phone to see if Eva was online. He wanted to apologise, but there were no excuses for his uncle's behaviour.

5.

Unable to settle, he gawked at the ceiling, wondering why Victor reacted angrily. What did he mean by her kind? Time drifted and the school day took forever to arrive. He picked at a bowl of cereal absentmindedly and spilled orange juice down his shirt. Scrolling through several messages, he dropped another apologising for his uncle's tantrum.

A reply arrived, and she agreed to meet after school, so they could hang out. Relieved they were on speaking terms, he charged his phone for the second time and walked to school.

Eva waited outside his classroom as her lesson finished earlier. He always crept out last, so she hid behind a wall, waiting. When he exited, she sneaked up, planting a baseball cap on his head.

"Get off me, or else!"

"Calm down, you'll send me flying again, Mr Angry."

He yanked off the cap, glancing at the Dolphin and baseball logo.

"What's this? I hate people touching my head, and hats."

"I think you look cute," said Eva, squeaking with delight. "It's time I introduced a proper game of sport, loved in every state!"

"I'm not cute, and the sports I play are proper sports. Football is a game of ultimate skill!"

She set the cap on his head again, adjusting it.

"Trust me, you won't encounter a sport more entertaining than baseball, a game designed for a crowd of over eighty thousand, it's mind blowing. Then there's the foot-long hot dogs with hundreds of toppings to choose from, yummy!"

Mikey's interest piqued.

"Where do we travel for said hot dog, I'm famished?"

"We catch a train to watch the Bridgeport Dolphins, they're top of the league. My dad brought me to see them when we first arrived, when they were a minnow team!"

"I don't have a change of clothes, other than my trainers. I'm stuck with this stupid uniform."

She threw over a light grey duffle bag.

"No drama, there's a baseball top and shorts, you'll be fine as it's humid today. I've got cash for the train and tickets for the game so you can repay me later!"

He looked at the baseball top, a climate-lite material like football jerseys from a well-established brand. The last sports memorabilia given to him came in the form of a signed shirt from a Bolton legend, Jay-Jay.

"This isn't as bad as I expected. I thought baseball tops looked like old referee uniforms, seems they improved the design. What time's the game on?"

Eva checked her pink flowery wristwatch.

"It starts at eight, so we've time to hang out. I'll tell you about the players, past and present!"

"Can't wait to hear about a sport I know nothing about."

The Bridgeport express wasn't faster as congestion doubled a twenty-minute journey. Track speed restrictions were in place because of the heat warping risk.

"How can you lose a massive stadium, are you lost?"

"No, we've taken the scenic route, honest."

"Scenic route? At one point I was ninety percent sure we'd get robbed. This part of town is terrifying!"

"In all fairness, it used to be worse and full of derelict factories, they've done loads. When they constructed the stadium, the place got regenerated except the area we detoured across."

"I'm pretty certain you got lost, admit it?"

"Maybe, but we found the stadium, look! Here, you'll need this ticket, scan it to get through."

They found entrance D and Mikey stepped towards the turnstile with his ticket ready to scan. In a little ticket box, the grumpiest woman he'd ever seen read a newspaper. When his ticket wouldn't scan, she snatched it from him, picked up her hand-held radio and said.

"Security to D, turnstile two, repeat security to D turnstile two!"

He searched for Eva, who'd already gone through the gate. He watched in horror as a security guard arrived.

"What's the problem, do we have another troublemaking punk?"

"This ticket's uplifted, there's two tickets on this account. Take them up, reception will deal with them."

The security guard glared at him in a way only someone official could.

"Is this your ticket, young man?"

Mikey eyed the six-foot seven giant, built like a brick house.

"Err, no. I mean yes, it's my ticket. A friend bought it for me, she's gone through the other gate next door."

"Follow me and point out your friend once we're inside."

What had she done, was the ticket real or did she purchase

fake ones? What did uplift mean? Through the turnstile, he pointed out Eva, and the man beckoned. Her face went white, and they trailed behind.

"Please tell me these tickets are real, I think we're in trouble?"

"Yeah, I bought them online, I swear. I picked them up from the booking office in downtown Milford. I don't understand why mine worked, and yours didn't?"

"No idea, but this guy is serious. The veins in his neck muscles are bigger than my arms."

They followed up several flights of steps to a set of blue double doors. The security guard held one open and escorted them inside. A marble reception desk took centre stage in a beautifully decorated room. The reception host smiled, but her look changed to a puzzled one.

"You two don't look so happy, but congratulations, we have selected your tickets in a prize draw for an executive box. You get to watch the match from your own personal space. They retail at over a thousand dollars for one game. Refreshments are all-inclusive, if you need anything ask!"

The guard held out his dustbin lid hand and shook Mikey's with such force; he wondered how his arm didn't get pulled off.

The host brought them to the executive box, right in the centre of the main stand. This view was perfect, positioned above the catcher's box. The game between the Bridgeport Dolphins and the Boston Beavers started soon. Mikey nosed around the box with its huge double balcony and concertina doors. Two blue leather recliner chairs sat in the middle with a huge flat screen TV positioned on the wall next to a refrigerator crammed with beverages. The TV showed the pregame with commentary and multiple angles of the field selectable by the user. To the right of the recliners, sat their very own hot dog cabinet and condiment table. Mikey pulled out the foot-long and placed it into a bun, topping it with onions, mustard, and tomato ketchup. The spiciness of the mustard and sweetness of the ketchup complimented the smoky flavour of the hot dog. He made another, passing it to Eva.

"Yuck, I hate onions, they are like slimy slugs on a plate."

"They are great, and that diner had one coated in batter called a blooming onion! Didn't think you were a Fussy eater?"

Mikey shovelled the second hot dog into his mouth, the happiest he'd been in weeks. He grabbed a root beer from the fridge and stepped outside to take in the environment. Noise from fans of all shapes and sizes in home and away kits filled the stadium. The teams took position, with Boston being first to bat, and the game started. It ended with Boston ahead of Bridgeport at seven to six. Eva booted a soda can outside the stadium.

"That's rubbish, the Dolphins should've won, that Boston player was out by miles!"

He struggled to understand how the game worked but put his arm around her shoulders.

"There's always the next game, that's what our coach said?"

"We needed the win and like always, we'll finish second as it's probably the Yankees year, again. Gonzales was in, he easily cleared the catcher by a foot!"

They exited the train and Mikey walked Eva home through the dark streets of Stratford.

"Thanks for inviting me to the game, I had fun. I'll wash these clothes and hand them back on Monday."

"Don't worry about the clothes, call them a gift, a welcome to town present. Thanks for walking me home."

She looked him in the eye's, entering his personal space and he panicked, patting her on the shoulder.

"Listen, my uncle's away on Tuesday, how about you come around and I'll show you the new games console he got? It's got amazing VR technology!"

Eva looked crestfallen.

"What about your uncle, last time, he was scary?"

"Don't worry, I'll sort it. I'll make sure he apologises, I think he had a bad day, that's all."

"Tuesday's cool, I suppose. Guess I'll talk to you then?"

"Don't be silly, I'll message you soon. I better get a jog on; it'll take ages to get home. Night Eva!"

She waved at the front door, closing it behind her. Alone in the street on his walk home, he had time to process what happened. He'd never panicked before. Confidence normally helped, but this time, with a girl he could be himself around, he became as shy as a snow leopard. The look of disappointment on her face made it obvious she liked him. Or did it?

Tuesday afternoon arrived, and he waited outside Eva's classroom at the end of last period. For once her class over ran, so he walked to his locker to store some books. When the locker door opened, a note drifted to the floor.

'Dear limey inbred, leave our school and take Skippy with you. America rules, England drools!'

He screwed up the note, throwing it into his locker.

"Aha, look here boys, the slimy limey got my note. Are

you gonna cry, you look like you gonna cry?"

Mikey faced three students. The anger inside bubbled to the surface. He never took abuse from anyone.

"Check out the poet! Rather be a slimy limey than a hillbilly inbred!"

The boy in the middle swung a punch in his direction and he dodged it, grabbing the boy's neck before he swung again. In the commotion, he hadn't seen the principal round the corner to an uninterrupted view. He signalled to break it up and directed Mikey to detention for causing an upset. A trail of laughs echoed through the corridor as he followed the sign to room '101' the school's detention centre. Before he entered, Mikey tried to text Eva to tell her he couldn't meet her, but his phone battery died.

The meanest looking teacher answered the door, pointing to an empty desk and white board with various rules.

Eva finished and searched the corridor where Mikey had been fifteen minutes before. Checking her phone, she saw the message about him depositing some books in his locker, but when she got there, the hallway was deserted. She strolled towards his house and let him know she'd meet there, taking a shortcut through the park. A juvenile Robin redbreast landed nearby.

The bird chirped and tweeted unphased. She called out and miraculously; it flew up, landing on her stretched-out hand, allowing Eva to pet it for a moment before flying away. Twenty minutes and four blocks later, she arrived at Mikey's house. A little annoyed he hadn't answered her messages, she sent one last text.

'I'm outside your house, you could read your texts. Answer the door, will you!'

She walked up the garden path past the old oak tree blocking off Mikey's bedroom and stepped up the creaky wooden stairs. Banging on the front door, she tried again when no one answered. Headed back up the path, Victor opened the door unexpectedly.

Taken aback by a girl he'd told never to visit, stood feet away. He fumbled with his ponytail.

"You knocked at my door girl, what do you want?"

"Mikey invited me, is he home?"

"With your mobile technology you would have communicated already?"

"He invited me, said you would be okay and that you'd had a bad day. You know, when you were awful to me?"

"I was awful to you, that's news?"

"Yes, you were awful, horrid in fact," said Eva, "I forgive you!"

Victor eyed Eva silently, the cogs in his head working overtime.

"Forget it. Sorry to waste your time, Mr Birt."

"Eva. Of course, he told me, I've got a memory like a sieve, old age for you."

She gauged his facial expression.

"Can you get him, please?"

Victor ushered her inside.

"Nonsense come inside. He is, err, inside doing dishes, hurry!"

He glanced down the street when Eva entered the kitchen.

"No one listens to Victor. I forbid him from seeing her, should've known he'd do the opposite, like me when I was his age. Well, say goodbye to Eva."

He smiled, took another look outside and closed the door.

6.

Two hours in detention felt like ten and when it ended, he gathered his books, swearing under his breath. He raced through the main gates into the park towards home, desperate to charge his phone and let Eva know what happened. In a daydream, he nearly tripped over a bench leg but rebalanced himself to avoid landing on a small elderly man perusing a newspaper.

"Wait, I recognise you. Where did you go?"

He vanished, but the newspaper remained neatly folded on the bench. Mikey shook his head and carried on to the house. The front door was slightly ajar, but his uncle never used it. Maybe Eva found the spare key to let herself in?

"Anyone home. Eva, you around, Uncle Victor, hello?"

Perhaps he'd left it open this morning.

When no one answered his calls, he placed his phone on charge, waiting for the compulsory ten-minute start up. A few messages came through, she wasn't happy being stood up. One last text arrived that said she had called by but went home annoyed. He messaged her several times, to no response.

Frustrated, he called her, hearing the same automated voicemail. He hadn't noticed Victor, who stood silently in the kitchen's corner until he glimpsed his reflection on his phone screen.

"You frightened the hell out of me, I thought you were

travelling out of town this evening to pick up a rare car?"

"I haven't left, had to fix up some urgent, paperwork."

"I'm going to be honest; I invited Eva over this evening. Save me the lecture on why she can't, she's my friend. Have you seen her, she knocked on the door?"

Victor ran both hands through his hair.

"No one knocked on the door today?"

"Have you seen her or not? If you were home, surely, you'd have heard the doorbell, the one that ding dong's through the house and nearly pierces eardrums?"

Victor pulled his face into a puzzled look.

"Can't say I have seen her, been home all day, no one knocked."

Mikey investigated his Uncle's face.

"The girl you barked at, the one you forbid me to see?"

Victor closed his eyes and shook his head.

"I remember her. You didn't listen to me, did you? Have you considered there's a reason I tried to stop you? To answer your question, I haven't seen her today, so enough of the third degree!"

Victor barked the last part, startling him.

"She's the nicest girl I know. I thought you were different. You and Dad are alike!"

Victor rattled pots and pans in the sink.

"Bolognaise for dinner, that sound good?"

Unable to get much from his uncle, he nodded to acknowledge bolognaise was fine, taking his phone upstairs. Eva was the one person he could be himself around. For the first time in his life, however unintentionally, he felt rejected. Letting out a frustrated deep breath when he saw his signal at zero, he threw the phone on the bed, making a mental note to track her at recess tomorrow.

The one time he fell asleep that night, he had a vivid nightmare. Hours felt like days inside a house with many doors leading to nowhere. A strange cloaked man wandered its corridors and a golden pocket watch ticked loudly in his pocket. He felt relief when the alarm sounded and, walking to school through the park, concentrated on the surrounding colours to block out the boys that followed. Yesterday wasn't a one off with the group shouting abuse and obscenities. Not keen for trouble, he scampered to school.

At his least favourite subject, maths, the teacher who never paid attention shouted.

"Michael Birt! The Principal wants to see you in his Office. Please follow Sam, she'll take you there."

He grabbed his things and tailed the girl. When they reached the office she walked away, nose in the air. He knocked and waited.

"Come in Mr Birt and close the door behind you!"

Mikey opened the door and stepped inside, taking in the scene. Two official looking people in black suits stood with their arms folded either side of the Principal.

"Hello Michael, the detectives have some questions for you, I hope you answer them quickly and return to class?"

Concerned, he nodded.

"I'm Detective Maxim and this is my colleague, Detective Dawson. I understand you were friends with a young girl by the name of Eva Lyfer?"

"What do you mean were friends!?"

The second officer looked at him.

"Bad wording, what my esteemed colleague meant is you are friends. Miss Lyfer didn't return home yesterday evening, and I understand you'd struck up a friendship?"

"Yes, detective, I was in detention when I meant to meet her after school. The Principal can back that up, he caught me fighting with a student."

Detective Dawson jotted down notes.

"When did you last see Miss Lyfer?"

"At lunchtime, recess, whatever it's called."

Detective Maxim interjected.

"We need details, full details, stop withholding information!"

He felt he'd entered a game of good cop, bad cop.

"Err, we spoke by text message, but I was in detention, like I said. She went to my house to call on me as my phone battery went flat, I assumed she went home annoyed."

"A likely story! You know what happened, don't you? It's suspicious you come over and befriend a girl, then she disappears, tell the…"

"Wow, calm down Maxim," said Detective Dawson, "she means well, we want to understand what happened."

"I'm worried too, I'll help if I can. Do you want me to send you the messages from my phone?"

"No, we can pull your phone records to confirm the last time you spoke. Did you say she went to your address to meet you?"

"That's what she said on her SMS."

"What's your address," said detective Maxim, "don't try none of this fake address crap either!"

"What's your problem? I'm cooperating. My address is on Spring Street off Bridgeport Avenue, you can't miss it, white picket fence and chain mail gate."

"Who do you live with, your parents?"

"I live with my uncle; he didn't hear the door. He should've been at work."

"Where does he work?"

Mikey remembered his uncle's car lot ceased trading.

"I'm not sure, he's out a lot, that's all I know."

Detective Dawson finished scribbling his notes and placed the notepad in his breast pocket.

"If we need to contact your uncle, is it best to get him at this address? Since you don't know where he works, can we contact him on a cell phone number?"

"He doesn't know how to use the landline and he's only got a TV because I'm with him, he's a real technophobe, his house is full of relics."

"Please ask him to call us, we can discuss Eva at his earliest convenience."

"I'll let him know you need to speak with him as soon as he's home, I can't say when that will be, he comes and goes a lot."

Satisfied with his responses, they handed a card over with their contact details, in case he remembered any information.

"Principal, would you mind if I went home? I won't be able to concentrate; this has upset me."

"Please go home and take some time to process today. If you remember any information, please let the detectives know. She is a student at this school. I don't want bad press. Please keep this to yourself. It would cause a frenzy if parents found out!"

The Principal only cared about the school's reputation, not for the safety of its students. Confused and upset at home, he picked up his phone, flicking back through the messages Eva sent. Desperate to get hold of her, he called her cell phone over and over. The distinct vibration of a phone on a wooden surface sounded through the hallway. He opened the bedroom door and called her phone again. The sound came from his uncle's bedroom, inside a chest of drawers. Opening each one, he found it. Why did Victor have Eva's phone?

7.

Mikey searched for Victor so he could explain why he had Eva's cell phone. Maybe he'd found it on the porch and that's why she hadn't answered him; but that didn't explain why she'd gone missing. Was his uncle responsible? He was eccentric, but would he stoop so low?

He dialled the detective's number, intent on informing them he'd found Eva's cell phone when the house rocked. He dropped under the bed, covering his head. The news mentioned an overdue Earthquake in the Tri-state area that could happen any day. His uncle said it was news for sheeple, but perhaps they were right. Pictures dropped from the walls; their frames smashed on the floor. It lasted around ten seconds and then halted. A noise like the crack of a whip filled the air and a red light appeared with the sound of frantic barks echoing through it. The light became blindingly intense, and he covered his eyes. The sounds stopped and Victor and Angus crashed to the floor.

He climbed from underneath the bed, and grabbing Eva's phone, backed against the wall.

"What happened to Eva! Did you drop from the ceiling? I imagined you both drop from the roof because I'm in shock, or I'm going insane. Why do you have Eva's cell phone? The police pulled me into the principal's office, asking questions. When were you going to tell me Brum motors shut!?"

"I didn't want you to worry, it's my burden. My father left me, and I tried to make a go of it. I never intended on running it into the ground, I didn't have time to run it. There are more important issues! I've made a cataclysmic mistake; I shouldn't have done it. We are in real danger and It's my fault. Please let me explain!"

"You're admitting you hurt Eva, what've you done to her!?"

"The black-eyed kids, the black-eyed kids, they're here. We're in danger; I did a stupid thing; I didn't expect this to happen. I tried to protect the world; she would have been okay!"

Mikey backed further into the corner, concerned by his uncle's mental state.

"Uncle Victor, tell me what you did!?"

"I made Eva disappear. You two shouldn't have met, we only ever hurt them. I sent her into another world and the black-eyed kids hitched a ride from the opposite side. They waited to enter an unguarded portal. They're here, because of my idiocy, we're all in danger!"

His father was right; Victor was dysfunctional.

"Listen, my father shut the black-eyed kids into Majjika. I didn't think they could escape, but they played us, waited for me to make one mistake and they took full advantage! Now I need your help!"

Mikey dialled nine, one, one. The operator asked if he required help. He tried to answer, but no words came. Victor grabbed the phone, ending the call, pleading with Mikey to listen. The lights flickered and pressure in the room built until a loud sound travelled through the house rattling the windows. Angus barked. Then it fell quiet. Victor slammed the bedroom door, holding himself against it.

The silence broke with the cruel cackle of laughter outside the front porch.

"Victor, oh Victor. Come and play, we know you're there. Come and play?"

"Too late, I'm too late. Arce and the others found me."

"Come on, play nice Victor," said the mischievous voice, "hand over the Veil and we'll leave you alone, we promise!"

"Mikey, I need to tell you something and it won't make any sense. I'm a reaper, I make sure the dead move on to what most call heaven. I help souls find their ultimate resting place. In return, I get power and immortality. I help govern the life and death ratio, for one to live one must die. We all have our time, even reapers to a degree, although we don't die unless taken by unnatural causes."

Victor caught his breath, then carried on.

"These creatures outside, yes creatures, want the Veil I wear. It governs the powers and allows me to swap between worlds. I can transport people, animals, and magical beings, etc. Those things outside are far stronger than me now. I tried to hold them off, but they found us, and they want the Veil. You must take it; they cannot get their hands on it. If they do, it will be disastrous."

Mikey squirmed on the spot, unsure what to believe. How could it be the truth?

"What am I supposed to do, I'm a teenage boy and you're a reaper, can't you reap them?"

"There are too many! Your grandfather locked them in Majjika. The other creatures there kept them in check. They didn't like it, but it worked, the worlds were better for it. They outsmarted us; I don't know how. All I know is because of me, we pay the price."

"What on Earth are you talking about, pay the price for what?"

"Take the Veil now; it hasn't chosen to move on, but you're next in line, I offer it to you. Put it on before it's too late!"

Victor pulled at his head and a black and silver Veil became visible. He grabbed at Mikey's hands and placed it into them. With one glance, he dropped it in confusion.

"I don't understand, black-eyed kids, what's going on, you're not making sense?"

A deafening rumble shattered the windows before he finished. They forced the front door open with such force; it shattered into pieces.

The cries outside sounded shrill and angry.

"You had your chance. You know it's impossible to beat us; we are far too powerful, hand over the Veil Victor!"

Victor picked up the Veil, passing it to him whilst waving his other through the air. A crimson light emerged in the centre of the room.

"I'll hold them off as long as I can! Rescue Eva, she's more important than I realised. I have no time to explain. Go through this portal. Locate Father Time and Mother Nature, persuade them to help, they'll know what to do!"

"Father Time, Mother, wait, unc…"

He shoved Mikey backwards into the portal and Angus howled as Victor picked him up and hoofed him in. The room vanished, but not before he glimpsed the door slam open. Sure enough, as Victor had outlined, three black-eyed kids ran through the doorway. They saw the Veil with Mikey, shrieked and raced toward the portal, but didn't reach it in time as it sealed.

They span out of control through the redness and dropped off into a deep black void. With no way to rebalance himself, he smashed into a dense oak table full of metal platters piled with food. The table collapsed, and the food passed into the air. His vision blurred, and his body ached as he took to his feet. The raucous music in the room ended. People occupied the room from wall to wall, each owned a pewter tankard. He doubled back. They weren't people at all. Three leprechauns, a selection of Fairies, a hairy goblin, a unicorn and man in tights with a bow and arrow, stood gawping, unhappy with the intrusion. The crowd changed from furious to fearful when they glanced at the Veil. The inn keeper pretended to wash a tankard with his back to the crowd.

"Pardon me, where am I?"

Mikey appealed to the inn keeper, who avoided his question, then to the leprechauns. When no one answered he questioned the man-like creature.

"You, fellow in tights with the bow where am I?"

"Leave me alone, it's not my time, I've done what you advised. Ask Victor, I'm a good cupid!"

"Either this is a daydream, or I've misplaced my mind. Can you please tell me where I am?"

"You're in Majjika, my inn more specifically. Your type ain't welcome around 'ere, if you've finished, sling your hook.

"Sorry, If I seem stupid, but where am I? None of you are human yet this feels real."

"Your far from Earth, that much I'll tell you. What your family did was inexcusable. Sending those, those things 'ere. Yeah, I know who you are. If you're 'ere, that means Victor's croaked it. He was all right, not his fault Charles was a complete moron!"

"You mean my grandfather, what did he do? Why's it difficult to get information?"

"I've told you; your lot aren't welcome, gallivanting around like you own the place, get out my inn!"

Mugs and plates flew in Mikey's direction. He bolted to the main wooden door in the corner, ducking as a mug skimmed his head, shattering against the wall. He fumbled at the catch as a turnip hit him square in the cheek, opened the door and departed.

8.

Daylight cascaded onto Mikey, blinding him for a moment. Outside the inn, a town not unlike a Mediterranean one looked dropped into the middle of an English countryside. The streets were narrow, with grey-white cobbled stones set along the pathway; the houses whitewashed, and stone faced, except for the inn, with its straw-thatched roof and timber frame. Colourful flowers protruded from baskets with a model village set between them. A small creature with wings stepped from one house.

"Goodbye love, see you when I return from work, if the boss doesn't work me to death."

Greeted by another creature, who kissed him on the cheek, he flew off. Mikey lightly slapped his face. This was bizarre.

The town sloped down towards a tremendous lake and beyond, a mountain range cut across the landscape perfectly. It created a breath-taking panorama, one of the most beautiful sights he'd seen. Engrossed in thought, he failed to spot a woman stood near a stone archway. She muttered to herself, and out of the blue, barked.

"Grow already!"

He snapped out of his thoughts. Her appearance was odd, she was easily one of the strangest people he'd seen. She wore long green robes with tree-like branches wrapped around and a three-pointed hat. A bonsai tree poked out the top. Its branches had an unkept look and its bark had a few scorch marks. The faint odour of fresh Earth and charred wood hovered around.

He approached carefully, not wanting to startle someone volatile. He needed to ask a few questions, even if this was some wild dream. The woman worked on a burnt tree husk. If he wasn't mistaken, she conversed with it. In between each word, she emphasised. Her stress became clear when she clapped her hands and lifted them into the air. The stump in front meandered its way up and grew inch by inch. All seemed fine, but as soon as it sprouted foliage, it stopped. She shouted and tapped her cane against the floor.

"Why won't you grow, why, why, why! Grow will you! Dear me, what have I done. Silly, silly me."

Several clouds blanketed the light and moved above the woman. They rumbled and grew darker. One powerful bolt of lightning shot directly at the stump, and then the clouds disappeared. Engulfed in a rage of fire, the woman screamed, trying to quell the flames with her hat.

"No, no, no, not again! My head's in the clouds, the clouds, I tell you. My poor tree, I'm sorry!"

He backed away, hoping the woman hadn't noticed him. With a huff and a puff, she yelled.

"This is your bloody fault! Do you realise the effort required to give life to a tree, a plant, a shrub? Do you know how much effort goes into repair work? If they die, you die!"

She lunged and walloped him with the cane, and he backed away.

"Lady, you're crazy! Back off!"

About to hit again, she stopped in her tracks at the distinct yelp of a dog. The innkeeper had Angus by the scruff of the neck.

"Get out of 'ere, stinky dog! Tryin' to piddle in my inn, go on sling yer hook. Oi you there, control yer mutt. Next time he tries that, 'e'll find 'imself on the other end of a barbeque, you 'ear me?!"

Angus ran towards him. Disgruntled, he snapped at his heels. Unsure of Angus, he asked him to sit and shockingly; he obeyed.

The woman froze.

"That's Victor's dog, he barely ever listened to him, always tried to erm, water my vegetable patch! If he's listened to you, then you've got that Veil. Oh, you do, I can see it in your hand. Shame, he was a good man."

"Who are you? How do you know my uncle?"

She looked puzzled. Then the penny dropped.

"You're Mikey! I'm Mother Nature, grower of flora and fauna and controller of weather, no one important."

"Mrs Nature, where am I, what's going on. Victor said I should find you?"

"It's Mother Nature. I've never married, and nor do I wish to. Such things are human constructs I don't conform to!"

"If you don't conform to such constructs, why is your name Mother?"

"You question my name?"

"No, I wondered why you're named that?"

"Why are you named Mikey? My name's Mother Nature, well Mother Nature the fifteenth, but that's beside the point!"

"You mean there were others named the same in your family?"

"Enough already, respect your elders! My names from a long line of ancestors. Yes, there were others."

"I need to find Eva once I locate Father Time, that is."

"Fantastic, ignore me and go straight for him. I could assist you better but never mind, be sexist, I don't care!"

"You've said your past human constructs, but now you're offended because I said I need to find Father Time?"

"The absolute cheek! A little recognition would be nice, that's all I ask!"

"Victor spoke of you," lied Mikey, "he mentioned you first. You were erm, his favourite, like an erm, mother to him!"

Mother Nature changed her demeanour and smiled.

"That's better, a bit of gratitude!"

"Yes, he said you were, erm, helpful and, erm, old."

"Well yes, I am helpful and, excuse me, old?!"

"I didn't mean old, I meant wise, intelligent, in touch with the world!"

"Ah, I'll let you off then. Old, that's the worst thing you could call a female. Just because I've seen two lifetimes, does not make me old!"

"You knew my uncle, and he knew you. You were close?"

"Victor and I go back to his teenage years. He had many questions too; seems the apple doesn't fall too far from the tree. My dear boy, Father Time, and I mentored him when he first took the Veil years ago. Before I reveal where you are, I'd put the Veil on, it's yours now."

He looked at the cloak, lifted and pulled it over his head. The world blurred and faded into black and white, then settled again. Angus self-combusted and Mikey used his hands and tried to put the flames out. The flames stopped as quick as they started. Where Angus the Rottweiler had been, now stood a husky.

"What the hell. Angus, is that you?"

73

Angus barked and jumped up to lick his face somewhat out of character.

"He's linked with the Veil, he is its protector, and as long as you wear it, he'll do so. Nothing will cause you harm, well mostly. There are exceptions to this rule; those black-eyed kids are immune. You're a reaper, you should be able to sense the life force of any creature alive. Those that suffer flicker, that means it's time for them to move on. Father Time is the exception, his life force alters. Under no circumstances, reap him!"

"So, I'm bad? I kill people?"

"No, you help them to their afterlife. You take them 'over the rainbow' to the ultimate resting place. You provide peace to those who suffer!"

He scratched his head. The Veil felt strange to him.

"One more question. Victor sent a girl here. Someone named Eva, then those black-eyed things got into my home and he sent me here. He said you and Father Time could help. He also said Eva's more important than he realised, and I kind of like her a lot."

"Yes, I knew all about that. Those evil little swine's hitch hiked a ride right to Earth on an unguarded portal from Majjika, courtesy of your uncle!"

"Erm, Majjika?"

"Your uncle didn't tell you about the oldest place in the known universe, Majjika? This world's for magical creatures of all shapes and sizes. We are free to do what we will, within the laws that govern us."

"You mean this is a different world? How is that even possible?"

"Not everything revolves around Earth, life exists

elsewhere!"

"I'm supposed to believe that there's a magical world and I'm not on Earth?"

"Believe what you want, but it won't change the fact you're here. It isn't a dream, you're in Majjika, the town of Penbridge to be exact. How else would you explain the portal?"

"Penbridge? You have names for places here too? I forgot to ask about the portal. How does that work?"

"We do, we aren't uncivilised cave people, dear. As for the portal, it's an ancient magic that binds our world to others. That's all I really know!"

"How many magical creatures are there, why aren't they on Earth?"

"Does the tooth fairy, Santa Claus, the Easter Bunny and cupid ring a bell? They all come from Majjika. Only certain creatures can go to Earth. A story for another time."

"How many creatures are there?"

"More creatures than insects on Earth. I don't know them all, I find a new one daily!"

"You're Mother Nature, don't you make them?"

"Dear boy, no, that was someone else's job, way before I arrived."

"Who created them?"

"Some say the original elder, before the council formed. Who knows, I never asked!"

"What about Majjika, does it have day and night, weather cycles, stars?"

"You have many questions, don't you? There's a day and night, dynamic weather changes and yes, stars. They are different to those on Earth. Each star is a piece of heaven for creatures that passed on."

"Thank you for the answers. Now have you seen Eva, you never said?"

She placed her hat on her head, looking at him through narrowed eyes.

"Yes, I saw her. I sent her toward Father Time. She wanted to get home; she wasn't from here. I helped her find the path and turned back. Don't look at me like that. If I looked after every stray, I'd get no work done, besides Father Time knows how to get her home, apparently!"

"Eva's not some stray, she's a wonderful human being, don't talk about her like that!"

She looked at him, peering into his eyes. It made him feel uncomfortable, as though she read every thought.

"I sent her towards the lake down a pathway named Creekstone Pass. Follow that, eventually you'll reach a crossroad, use the right path and it'll lead you to Father Time's manor."

"Can't you come with me; I could do with help?"

"You have your directions to the Manor, that's as much help as I can be, I'm too busy to gallivant!"

"Why is everyone terrified of me? The people in the inn went ballistic?"

"Isn't it clear you're a reaper? Not every creature that has a failing life force wants to depart. In fact, some will actively avoid you, you'll discern that with time!"

"Thank you, I suppose, though I still have no idea where I am."

She pointed to the pathway, and he set off down the hill with Angus.

9.

At the foot of the hill, he followed a mossy cobblestone path stretching for miles along the shoreline. The lake was monumental, its blue water shimmered, reflecting the light. It called out, as most water did. Normally he'd dive in, now wasn't the time. He reached a darkened tunnel which led away from the shoreline and with no alternative route he entered. Damp and boggy, the ground squelched and cold water soaked into his shoes and socks. Angus trotted past, nearly bowling him over, and shook water everywhere.

"Cheers for that, silly dog!"

The tunnel took time to navigate owing to poor light. On the wall to the left, he touched a slimy section, recoiled in disgust and wiped his hand on his pants. On the other side, he removed his shoes and tipped the water out, wrung his socks, then dried his feet. In a steep valley headed downhill, he rounded a corner and reached a fork and assessed his options. There was a commotion ahead as Angus barked, and a voice shouted.

"Get off mi eggs, you big brute, get off I say, they're mine, not yours, I worked hard to make these. I'm not afraid of you, I'll fight you if I have too. Right then, don't say I didn't warn you, you asked for this, stupid mutt!"

He rushed around the corner to a full view of the largest bunny rabbit he'd seen. She kicked Angus square in his face whilst trying to arrange what looked like chocolate eggs back into a basket.

"Angus, stop it at once, leave the eggs, they don't belong to us, they are the property of this creature, behave!"

Angus lay on the ground sulking, paw over his face as dogs do when in trouble.

The bunny took one look at Mikey, registered the Veil and shrieked.

"You won't take me anywhere without a fight, no way a reaper's taking me, not today, you keep your grubby mitts of me!"

"Wow, calm down, it's okay, I won't hurt you, I want to ask you a couple of questions, please Sir?"

"You dare assume I'm male? The Easter Bunny is always female. Sir, the sheer cheek of it!"

Mikey stumbled, and the bunny jumped back, shocked at his sudden movements. He plucked up the eggs, which included a golden one, depositing them into the basket.

"I didn't mean to offend; did you say you're the Easter Bunny, as in the bunny in the stories our parents mentioned as kids?"

She scoffed as he picked up the basket, holding it out. She reached out and snatched it away, hopping off.

His voice echoed into the distance as he called after her, and his pleas sounded desperate.

"Sorry I offended you! Where is Father Time's? Please help!"

She surveyed Mikey, then hopped toward him.

"Cause you were nice, and I'm not in the mood for a fight today, I'll help you. Father Time's house is on my route. If you can keep up, you're welcome to tag along. Your dog's eating chocolate, they aren't s'posed to!"

Sure enough, Angus had tucked into a stray egg.

"Naughty dog!"

Angus licked his paws.

"If you get sick, don't blame me, you're not supposed to eat chocolate!"

He followed, but it was tough. She bounded ahead, shouting for him to keep up. In-between breaths, he asked questions on the way to Father Time's. Perhaps he could find out if anyone spotted Eva.

"Have you seen a girl with thick curly hair and brown eyes, smaller than me, called Eva?"

She hopped excitedly.

"I did, and she was lovely. Unlike present company, she recognised I was female, I helped her locate Father Time's, funnily enough. He hasn't had proper company in years, he's going to go bananas!"

She hopped off, and he sprinted to keep up, grateful for the breaks as she deposited eggs into little holes in the ground. The last one they reached seemed bigger. It had a door decorated with pictures of elves and an inscription. She placed the eggs next to the door and rang a little bell. A short while later a small elf popped out in green and red, grabbed the eggs and disappeared. He wanted to ask a question, but she answered before he could utter a word.

"This is helper's hole, where Santa's elves' work. The words translate to little helpers of Santa, or rather, Santa's little helpers. I dropped some well-earned snacks off. They get overworked, poor buggers. I remember when the population was half what it is, and they worked a month of the year, now's its twenty-four seven work, all year round!"

The scene felt dreamlike, yet the plethora of smells confirmed it as real.

"You're an odd reaper, first one I've met with manners."

"You keep calling me a reaper, but I've reaped no one and my uncle pushed me into this world, I have hurt no one, I swear!"

"Don't talk about Victor Birt the clueless. By clueless, I mean off the charts clueless!"

He got the distinct impression no one liked his uncle in Majjika. After a brief pause, she continued.

"I'm not fond of him, he's clueless to our needs, only cares about Earth. I guess that's all Birt's for you, so self-absorbed in their work, they forget to care for others!"

"When I entered this world, I crashed onto a table at the inn in Penbridge, I interrupted a party, why?"

"Folks think it's time for celebration, and I can't blame them, but those horrible demonic buggers will be back, I guarantee it. We've spent decades trying to control them and keep them from trouble, so long in fact we forgot to live our own lives. They corrupted some of our kind in the early days. Paranoia set in and a lot distrusted each other. Even now they're elsewhere, I'm sure we haven't heard the last of them."

She paused, then continued with the same hushed tone.

"Those evil kids, whatever you call them, the things that were here. I doubt they have gone for good; they wanted Majjika and Earth to be one. They wish to control it all. We blame your grandfather for them in Majjika. I know he had no choice. Maybe you can see why no one likes reapers?"

"My grandfather, as in Charles Birt of Connecticut?"

"I fear for Earth. Wherever they have gone, whatever they are up to, it only means trouble. We are a magical world; we can hold our own. Humans however cannot, they do not understand what's on the horizon once they dig their heels in!!"

A group of fairies cut across their path and pointing at the Easter Bunny, they broke into chorus.

"She's small and mini, Fluffy yet fickle, the Easter Bunny's the real deal. She'll bound and hop, puff on the spot, she'll shout, she'll squeal, and I'll tell you what, can she tell tall tales!"

"Everyone," piped up the leader, "the Easter Bunny is telling tales again, ha-ha!"

They waved their tiny wands, and streams of scalding water and sparks flew toward her. She hopped on the spot, trying to swat the fairies with her paws. She pointed up to a steep hill and a pathway that meandered into the cloud line.

"Stop it, you little blights! I can't deal with this! Take the four thousand steps to the top, you'll reach Father Times manor!"

She hopped off into the distance and Mikey lost sight almost immediately. The fairies laughed hard, then looked at him and the Veil. The laughs changed to screams as they scattered in different directions.

"Not me, please, I'm too young to die, I've loads to live for!"

Mikey shrugged and turned to the four thousand steps, absorbing the sheer steepness of the climb ahead.

"Oh, that's steep, I hope the bunny was right. Four thousand steps! Angus, you ready?"

He looked at the steps, let out a sigh of protest and bound ahead. After the first hundred, they were already out of breath.

He tried to break down the steps into tens, so it would

seem less painful, but changed his mind and counted as many as he could. After a thousand, he checked their progress. Not one for heights, he held on to the iron rails. Although secure and well-built, they made him nervous. Over the rail, an enormous drop awaited anyone unlucky enough to stumble.

"There isn't a manor in sight, I've lost count now. Can't be much further, surely?"

Angus shook his head, as if to disagree, then carried on the upwards slog.

He felt lightheaded from how far up they were as the cloud line appeared, and they walked into a dense fog. Moisture from within the clouds dampened Angus's fur and Mikey's clothes as they made their way further up. The cloud cover cleared, and they reached the last steps of the four thousand. A rooftop came into view. This was Father Time's manor, a most peculiar house.

10.

The courtyard walls surrounding the manor had different clock faces at intervals. Some moved fast, some slow. Some moved backwards and forwards. A distinct Tick-Tock started as he approached the gate. Mikey tried to push it, but it locked into place. He tried to climb over but slipped down. The walls were high and covered in spikes. The gate had a tiny clock, and he reached out, turning the hands anticlockwise.

"Who dares disturb me at this hour!"

The clock grew until it consumed the gate. Two huge wooden doors appeared underneath the clock face. The doors rattled and then with no notice, a giant cuckoo bird popped out. Mikey jumped back several feet and manic laughter filled the grounds. The laughter carried on until Angus leapt forward and attacked the giant fake bird. Springs, cogs and feathers flew everywhere. The head detached, rolling downwards, and the laughter changed to an angry bark.

"My precious cuckoo! Do you know how priceless one is?! You'll pay for that! My wonderful, wait, that dog acts like, although it cannot be, unless. Don't you move, I'm on my way out, you can explain to me why you have Victor Birt's dog!"

The doors of the cuckoo clock shrank into the gate. A wall rose into the air and two heavy ironclad doors appeared. A clink and clank of chains and locks filled the air. One or two more clicks later, the doors opened outwards. Smoke filled around him and it was a few seconds before his eyes adjusted. He covered his face and pulled up his t-shirt, then walked forwards. He appeared from within the smoke, looking livid. His appearance amused Mikey, he was less than five feet tall. He looked at Father Time, who wore a black suit with a printed white clock face. His red and black shoes were clown like with a clock theme on each toe cap. Even his tie had a time related quote. The smoke cleared, revealing a courtyard and the front walls of the manor. It was humongous, or Father Time tiny.

Mikey fought to keep his face straight and diverted attention to Angus, who'd sneaked into the courtyard. He reached a limestone statue of a tall man with a pocket watch, took one look, then cocked up his left leg.

"No matter how quick you think you are, so much as sneeze near that statue of my father, and I'll castrate you faster than you can shake a paw!"

Angus realised he was serious and put down his leg begrudgingly.

Mikey struggled to keep a straight face, the overwhelming feeling of the situation hard to fight off.

"What's your problem boy, why do you look like you're about to laugh, spit it out?"

He laughed, and it took a good thirty seconds to calm down. He motioned with his hands to reference how tiny he was.

"Yes, all right, I get it, I'm not very tall. Hilarious, ha-ha. You think, big voice, tiny man. Haven't you ever heard; big things come in small packages?"

"I'm, ha-ha, sorry," said Mikey in fits of giggles. "You're the height I was when I was five!"

"I know who you are! You have the cheek of someone

that's been a thorn in my side. Didn't recognise you at first, you looked different in bed asleep!"

"Different in bed, you watch me sleep?"

"I saw you at your uncle's. You were asleep in his old room. Who do you think helped sort that dump of a house out?"

"You're the little man I saw in the doorway? Come to think of it, I saw you in the park, reading a newspaper. I doubled back. And you'd gone. I thought I'd imagined it!"

"Yes, it was me! I had instructions to watch you whilst your uncle attended to other areas of business as apparently, I have no life!"

Mikey scratched his head and murmured.

"Something happened back at my uncle's in Milford. There were strange black-eyed kids, only they weren't kids. He sent me to find Eva, Victor sent her by accident, I think."

"I told Victor it would be a matter of time before they escaped. Like his father, he never listened."

"Whatever those things are, they've got him. He sent me to find Eva and I'm here to get her home. Where is she?"

"You weren't supposed to meet Eva! Perhaps in time that'll become clear to you. I sent her away with a map and plenty of rations, to the wells of Nymphoria. It's the only way for humans to get home. Victor shouldn't have sent her here; she wasn't ready for our world."

"What do you mean she wasn't ready?"

"Never mind, some things are best left for Victor to explain, I'd rather not get involved, thank you."

He clenched his hands into fists, punching the wall closest to him.

"It's Mikey! I don't use my full name! Tell me what you

mean, I'm frustrated?!"

"I don't shorten names, nor do I appreciate your attitude. Respect your elders!"

Mikey cursed under his breath.

"Speak up boy, I didn't quite catch that!"

"Um, I'm sorry."

He nodded in acceptance, glancing at his pocket watch.

"Thank you. If you've finished with the insults, come in. They say my manors the best one here, all I know is, it's got the best time-keeping by a country mile!"

Not about to push his luck, he followed through the oak double doors. Statues shadowed the corridors with their silhouettes, doors of different sizes scattered around the hall, and pictures with numbers and strange symbols sat framed along the walls. He wanted to enquire about the manor's history, but time was precious.

"What are those black-eyed kids, what exactly are they?"

"The black-eyed kids are part of a few creatures that spoil it for the rest. They were terrible eggs and used deception to cause mayhem. For that, we locked them in a magical prison."

"Where is this prison, why aren't they in it?"

"The prison is in Majjika. Someone unlocked the gate, or they escaped without the need to open it. Perhaps no one helped them, who knows."

Mikey thought monsters only existed on television.

"I know what you wish to ask, I don't know who would help them out. I have suspicions on how they escaped, each guess as wild as the next."

"How did they escape this prison, one of the guards would have noticed them vanish?"

"My best guess is they tricked someone within the council

of Majjika or they had a way to detect new portals within Majjika. When the portal opened and Eva arrived, they slipped through the opposite side hitching a ride to Earth."

"Why did no one attempt to stop them?"

"No one in Majjika would allow them to leave without a fight, I am one hundred percent certain of that."

"Why did no one believe it possible if these creatures are as powerful as they sound?"

"It's against our known laws and rules as portals are one way. They discovered how to override it, and no one knows how, not myself nor the council of Majjika."

"Council of Majjika?"

"They oversee Majjika. They serve a similar purpose to the MP's you have back home, only they're elected every three years. It's supposed to keep the politics fresh. Perhaps so no one has time to ruin the hard work done by others."

"I don't understand politics, everyone argues over it."

"The black-eyed kids made life hell. Most creatures were glad they disappeared. How did you and Eva meet?"

"I moved with my uncle Victor after trouble back in England."

"I already know that boy, I helped your messy uncle fix the damn house up. How did you cross paths?"

"I travelled into town for a uniform and bumped into her, apologised and we got talking, kind of hit it off."

"I see, I see."

"What do you see!?"

"Does Victor know you befriended her?"

"He found out when I invited her around. He kicked her out, I think he had it in for her because she's an Aussie, he hates people out of town."

"What's an Aussie?"

"Aussie is short for Australian; she was born there. What's with the clocks?"

"Each of them represents a version of the past, the present and the future. There're several worlds and an infinite number of time zones you can go forward and backwards in, provided the world exists."

"You mean there is a master watch that can control time? Sounds like a series on TV back home called Bernie's watch."

"I'll show you. Stand next to me."

He pulled out his golden pocket watch, opened the glass cover and turned back the hour and minute hands. A strong wind filled the room, and it darkened. The only light came from Mikey's LED wristwatch. The wind stopped, and the light returned to the room, Father Time disappeared. A second later, he heard his voice. Father Time and Eva stood together.

"Now Emma, please calm down, I'm sure we'll get you home."

"My name's Eva, not Emma, and I can't calm down, I have no idea where I am!"

"I misheard. It's not as bad as it seems, I'm sure there's an explanation to why you're here?"

"Yes, Victor Birt tricked me. He invited me into his home and then some strange lights appeared around me. I felt a shove and fell on a table in some pub!"

"Victor sent you to Majjika?"

"He's the one who shoved me through. I span around, vomited, and ended up in this place, Majjika?"

"A world for magical creatures, like me. You know what Victor is?"

"Yeah, an evil man. I want to go home!"

"How did you come across my manor," asked Father Time, "who sent you?"

"Mother Nature, and I can't quite believe this, but the Easter Bunny helped."

"Why did Mother Nature send you to my manor, how did she know I'd even be home today?"

"She said you had a map and a shortcut to Nymphoria?"

"If you get the once a week ship on the shore of Lake Majji before nightfall, you'll save time."

"I don't understand, there're magical creatures and an entire world that isn't home?"

"This place is real Eavy, let me assure you of that!"

"It's Eva. How can I get anywhere, I have no money?"

"Your money will be no good. Take this bag. The crystalis will act as currency. It should get you on the ship and purchase a few supplies. I can provide you with rations and a map."

"You'll come with me and help, won't you?"

"I cannot escort you; I am far too busy working on a project with a friend right now."

Mikey fought back the guilt that crept through every bone. No matter what, he needed to get Eva home. He wondered how to approach and decided carefully was the best way. He cleared his throat and moved toward her. Eva didn't react. He attempted to get her attention by waving his hand in front of her face. She didn't react until Father Time pointed out of the window to the distant mountain range. He handed her a map and what looked like rations of food wrapped into little parcels. Eva loaded them into a blue backpack and made her way out the front entrance, thanking him. With a nervous look, she headed through the courtyard. The door shut and relief spread across his face. He walked to Mikey and pressed the stem on his watch.

"I followed what I did down to the last detail. Had I not, it could have resulted in another parallel timeline. Trust me, that's the last thing we want. Another set of those black-eyed kids terrifies me. I had to stop you being visible, so you couldn't interact."

"Why," said Mikey exploding with anger. "Couldn't you let me go with her to the wishing wells!"

"I don't expect you to understand. I could not allow you to interact. If any detail changed, you would have ended up on another timeline."

"What are you on about!?"

"If you bumped into another you, it could cause all kinds of issues and however small the chance, it isn't worth the risks associated."

"I don't understand, why would it matter if I helped her now rather than later. You interacted with her, what did you do with the other you? Where did the other Father Time go?"

Father Time lowered his head into his hands, speaking through them.

"I'm the only one in existence that isn't present in every timeline. I'm always me, there're no doppelgangers. Let's move to your timeline, so you can be on your way."

He moved the watch hands forwards, and the room reappeared as before. Father Time ushered him to follow through the manor and didn't say a single word. It was a strange place, he wondered, if it was Father Time's personal design? The walls were bright purple and black. He followed into a large corridor. There were no floors, instead a series of clock faces in-between a void into nothingness. Father Time looked at him.

"It appears I may have set off the manor security system. I'll admit, when I put it into place, I was much nimbler and able to hop and jump my way around these clocks. Now I am far too inflexible. Please deactivate the alarms on the other side. The floor needs resetting."

Mikey looked at the sheer drop on either side of the clock faces. One mistake, one slip, it was over. Angus cowered behind a brown chesterfield sofa to the side of Father Time. Knowing he was the only one that could, he faced the clocks.

"You designed everything in this manor, surely you created a work around?"

"I helped design it, went slightly overboard. Good luck!"

He took a deep breath and jumped onto the first clock face. A silver and black one. It made a distinct Tick-Tock noise and vibrated. It became difficult to balance. Three uneven steps later, he jumped onto the next face and skipped across. Two faces down, three to go. The next one had bigger hands. To make matters worse, they moved in opposite directions. If the hands moved to where he stood, they'd shove him over the edge. He jumped to the next clock, a red and a black one with a trap door. The door popped open and out came a king's guard with a sword. It stood frozen in place. He stepped forward, and the guard threw the sword into the air which crashed down with such force, it rocked the face. The guard lifted the sword again, and he jumped to the next clock face. A yellow and a black one. The guard vanished, and the hall fell quiet, too quiet.

An unmistakable buzz filled the hallway and echoed through the darkness. Black and yellow meant one thing in Mikey's head, wasps. The swarm made a bee line for him. His cry turned to a scream, and he dropped off the edge.

"No, what have I done!" Father Times voice echoed, and the hallway went quiet. He peered over the edge and caught sight of Mikey, who barely held onto another clock face. "I thought I'd killed you. Are you okay?"

To Mikey's sheer luck, the last clock moved backwards and forwards and was under the other when he slipped. He grabbed hold for dear life. Once his hands were secure, he heaved himself up. The shock meant it took a few moments to focus on the hallway.

"Yeah, I'm okay. Meant to do that, obviously!"

The clock face shuddered as he approached the other side. He stepped onto solid ground and not a moment too soon. The clock face flipped over and dropped into the void below.

Father Time cheered and shouted across.

"Well done! Under the grandfather clock, locate and pull the lever near the pendulum, not the other, that will send you goodness knows where!"

He pulled then pushed it down with force. The floor vibrated, and the walls shook as it rose from the void below. A clatter and click signalled it locking into place. Father Time hurried across and clapped him on his back.

"Couldn't have done it better myself, well done. I particularly liked when you fell off, had me worried you'd met your untimely demise. How to trick an old man!"

"It was all part of the plan, honest!"

"I knew it, you little trickster!"

"What other surprises do you have in terms of security?"

"An alarm that triggers a swarm of killer bees, a trip wire that releases man-eating beetles. There's booby-trapped doors that open on a wild ride to nowhere, and a few other features I'll keep secret!"

"Are the other things worse than man-eating beetles, wasps and guards with swords?"

"They may be as torturous. Super courageous Angus can come out from behind the couch!"

Mikey looked to Angus; half hidden behind the couch.

"It's a few clocks, get a grip."

"Correct me if I am wrong here, but don't canines dislike vacuum cleaners, hairdryers, showers, even their own shadows?"

"It's true! I suppose I expected more when, a few weeks ago, he pinned me in a corner. If I'd have known he was this soft, I'd have booted him out of the room!"

"He's soft now, but when it matters, he'll be there to protect you. With his life, if needed."

"Really?"

"You are keeper of the Veil; his job is to protect you and he'll do that come what may."

Mikey didn't want to think of any animal hurt.

"I'm not keeper of the Veil, my uncle is."

"For now, it's you, and will be when his time comes."

"If I don't wish to be next in line?"

"You have no choice, it's in your blood as the oldest male. Your uncle sired no offspring."

Mikey pulled the Veil; it was uncomfortable. Father Time beckoned further down the corridor, through a door. As soon as it looked like they reached the end, another corridor popped up. The last one seemed smaller, dedicated to a single door. A plaque on it read 'the grand library.' Father Time held open the door and invited him in. With no time to react, something flew overhead and caught Mikey. It left two or three deep scratches. He bawled out and Angus barked, jumping into the air at something which screeched. Mikey placed his hands to the back of his head. Whatever hit him had drawn blood.

"Ouch, Angus, quiet, I can't hear myself think!"

Angus moved into the corner to sulk. The distinct sound of a bird of prey called from overhead. On one of the timber rafters sat a bald eagle. Father Time mistook his look for interest.

"Isn't she beautiful?"

They had different ideas on beautiful.

"She is majestic if I say so myself. Bertha is fifteen pounds and her wingspans seven feet. She can fly one hundred miles per hour on a downward glide and is one of the fastest creatures."

"How did you find her?"

"She was a few days old when I found her abandoned on the ridges of Mount St Helens in Washington. I was with your, I mean, an old friend on a hike, when I stumbled across her!"

"Who did you hike with?"

"Well, I was on a hike with a man I miss dearly. He wasn't dissimilar to you in his early years. As for Bertha, she's an American bald eagle, a symbol of the United States!"

"You didn't answer my question. Who did you hike with?"

"The simple answer is, it's not of your concern who my friend was."

Father Time called Bertha. She floated onto his shoulder with surprising accuracy. She wasn't much smaller than him. Given half the chance, would she carry him away for dinner? The talons that gripped onto his shoulder made Mikey vow not to annoy her. Should they ever meet again?

"I need to find Eva, can you help?"

Father Time nodded and beckoned him to the window. He pointed out to the hills and mountains in the distance that were visible. Now the cloud cover had cleared.

"It won't be a straightforward journey. It involves a thousand miles of land and sea. A large portion will be on foot."

"Okay, I should get going. Any idea where I should start?"

"Before leaving, perhaps have a drink. You look tired, that Veil can be an enormous burden to bear. Let me fix you a hot beverage?"

He disappeared into a kitchen within the library.

11.

Mikey sniffed the drink, turning his nose up. The scent reminded him of sweaty socks. Father Time watched eagerly and not wishing to offend, he sipped, pleasantly surprised.

"It tastes better than it smells. I've never consumed a drink before that smelled awful yet tasted delicious."

"I assume by that statement you like it?"

"Tastes similar to cream soda mixed with butterscotch and salted caramel."

He disappeared, returning with a glass jug of a substance that looked like clouds. It swirled, and he swore a flash of lightning illuminate the liquid.

"This is an incredibly popular beverage in Majjika that every magical creature consumes to recharge their batteries. We aren't like humans. Did you notice your uncle rarely slumbered?"

"I haven't slept since Connecticut, put it down to jet lag and nervousness at school, now it makes sense."

"The Veil prevents sleep. It provides the wearer an amount of magic, you can reach heaven and back. Yes heaven exists, another story for another time."

"My uncle could come and go as he pleased?"

"Under normal circumstances you can skip between worlds, but those black-eyed kids locked us out. The only option is via the manual gate at the wishing wells of

Nymphoria."

"Have my family always been reapers?"

"Sixteen generations. The oldest male of the family line takes over."

"Why not a female that's a bit sexist, isn't it?"

"We didn't set the rules, they were made before our time by an unknown third party, possibly death himself. No one really knows, we follow the rules, in case Death ever returns."

"Will he be alright without the Veil?"

Father Time investigated his cup like the most interesting object he'd ever seen.

"I don't have the answer you seek; I can only cross my fingers."

"What ingredients go into the drink, what's it produced with?"

"It's named Pilichee. The original elders of Majjika created a concoction all could drink. Creatures passed prematurely, not ideal for a world reliant on magical longevity, so they acted and did something. It's an energy drink for Majjikans, and only one family knows the secret recipe."

He downed it, feeling alert. The sound of his phone's low battery alert jogged his memory.

"Help me locate Eva, please, I need all the help I can get?"

"She's ahead, and the path to Nymphoria laden with surprise."

"Eva didn't leave long ago; I might catch her if I get a jog on."

"Catching her won't be an easy feat. Four hours is one hour on Earth. By my calculations Eva has been gone three days in your world, twelve days here."

"Please tell me you had her accompanied on her journey?"

"I sent her with a map and food parcel, I've been snowed under with research."

"It's settled, you're coming with me, pack your bags."

Father Time stopped petting Bertha.

"I don't have time to hold your hand and navigate, I'm a busy person!"

"Scaring people at the gate with your booming voice and cuckoo bird, sounds like busyness to me?"

Father Time stomped, startling Bertha, who flew toward the roof rafters.

"Listen, boy; because of you, she's in Majjika! I'm not required to do anything, thank you!"

"Angus, piddle on everything, Father Time's got an attitude problem."

He trotted to the nearest statue, cocking his leg.

"I'll make you a lady dog, don't push me Angus Birt!"

Angus didn't listen, releasing a steady stream of urine.

"He listens to me. You sure you won't help; I've heard the acidity of urine can dissolve limestone?"

"This is outrageous, damn right ridiculous, the sheer audacity of the situation!"

"If I'm a reaper, maybe your times come, though I may be persuaded to err, keep you alive as Victor had an agreement I'd hope to keep."

"You c-c-can't reap me, me! How dare you threaten me! Are you serious, you, scoundrel? I'm required to help, but I warn you, I do under duress!"

He climbed a chair into a cupboard, speaking to himself in a hushed tone.

"The sheer cheek, threatening me, who does the boy think he is, coming into my home on an unsolicited visit, expecting the world to bend over backwards!"

He rummaged around, dropping several food packages, jumping off the chair with a thud. Mikey wondered how someone tiny could make a racket.

"Follow me and no questions please, I'm not in the mood to relinquish any answers!"

They walked through another hallway in silence. Mikey took in strange sculptures and pictures. They all held the same pocket watch. The hallway sloped downwards, and he crouched to avoid hitting his head. Father Time stopped in front of an antiqued grandfather clock, pulling open its glass door.

"Stand back a smidgen, this hasn't operated since I was a whippersnapper!"

The floor rumbled, and a bell chimed, like the warning sound of a level crossing. The noise halted, and the clock creaked and groaned, then split in the middle. It stopped with a clunk, leaving an enormous gap. A few steps were visible down a black tunnel.

"This clock is special, hand built by my late father and me. The wood is from a little-known tree with bark so thick it takes diamond to cut it. The pendulum is constructed of a rare metal element from a curious place named Fataportas, by a clock maker in a mountainous village only accessible one month a year."

"Wonderful, another dark dangerous place to explore, I can't wait, honest."

"This tunnel is another project I constructed with my father when I was a boy. Took months to create with blood, sweat and tears and the amount of rubble alone from its construction, helped shore up the foundation for the extension of the manor. Aren't you interested where it goes?"

He investigated the hole but couldn't see more than a couple of steps. A damp, Earthy smell and echo of a drip sounded from within. Angus made a beeline for the hole and Mikey grabbed his collar.

"Your cellar? Perhaps a deep dark dungeon you throw those you dislike?"

"Nope, a tunnel right to the lake shore."

"Another four thousand steps, fantastic, as if my legs didn't hurt enough!"

"You think I'd traverse four thousand steps down a mountain! It's one hundred steps, a hop, skip and jump, down a few flights of stairs and bingo; we'll be out in no time. Let's get this show on the road, follow me!"

He ducked, following into the tunnel, descending the first few steps as darkness engulfed them. Feeling the side of the wall as they navigated forward, surprised the walls were smooth and cold, like the feel of marble. The steps narrowed as they approached the final few, and he tripped.

"Are you okay? Do you want me to turn on the light?"

"There's a light, and you didn't turn it on?"

"To be fair, you never asked."

A distinct clink sounded, and the tunnel glowed orange. As Mikey suspected, the walls were marble. They looked smooth and perfectly carved. Magic had to be involved, he couldn't see Father Time doing manual labour. They walked for a few minutes until ahead the natural flow of daylight entered through a translucent gap in the stone face. Father Time walked straight through the other side and beckoned him to follow. He took one deep breath and followed through the gap. The strangest sensation washed over him, like walking through wallpaper paste. On the other side, he brushed himself off, amazed his clothes were bone dry. He faced the gap, but it disappeared. Father Time noticed the look of amazement on his face.

"The wonders of our world! This concealed entrance is the piece de la resistance to our construction, my old man gloated for months on completion!"

Mikey focused his attention toward the great lake. The light glistened and cascaded across the surface. Below, strange colourful fish swam in schools. The lakebed had the smoothest sand he'd seen. Behind them, they could make out the clock tower of the manor. They travelled quite a distance in a brief space of time. Perhaps this wouldn't be difficult.

12.

Father Time strolled to the shoreline, dropping his pocket watch into the water.

"No, your watch!"

"Not my precious watch. What will I do without it!"

"I can't believe you dropped it; how could you be so careless?"

He didn't reply, watching the water with a blank expression. He squeaked a sound of delight at the sight of an enormous bubble.

"Here we go, let's see if it worked!"

A huge bubble surfaced, causing a ripple effect across the shore. They grew in volume until the water bubbled. A few pops and glugs revealed a periscope, then a submarine emerged. Angus backed away, barking wildly.

"Where did the sub come from?"

"The master watch can become any object as long as it cannot harm others. With this sub we should be able to travel without detection. We must avoid the risk of unwanted attention."

At the invitation of Father Time, he stepped onto the platform and lowered Angus down the ladder, then followed. The hatch locked into place, revealing a far larger sub than seemed possible from outside.

"How is this possible?"

"Magic, Michael, magic!"

He stepped up to the main control panel with intent on his face, his tongue poking from the side of his mouth. He pressed buttons, scratched his head, made a few erms and not much else happened.

"Would you like a hand?"

"No thank you, I shall get it started don't worry. It's been a while since I've had to do things, manually."

Mikey looked at the control panel.

"Press this, pull that lever there, and see, it's started in no time."

A bright flash preceded a bang, and the engine roared to life.

"Back in my day, things were simpler. You didn't have these technical doodads. The older I get, the quicker the world drifts away from me."

"Where are we heading? What's with the sub?"

"Normally, I can teleport anywhere. Because they disconnected the magic of our world, I'm required to operate things, manually."

"Why's it disconnected?"

"Hard to say. My guess is a magical lockdown on our world. Perhaps to protect us, perhaps to keep us locked away."

"Why this form of transport?"

"To get across the great lake undetected, we must use this mode of transport. You must understand, I power it from my life force. I require a recharge around the halfway mark. There is an underwater city named Majji, full of wonder and charm. If you're not careful, it will swallow you whole. We stop at nightfall and continue once I've recharged."

"Correct me if I'm wrong, but underwater city?!"

"Full of things you'll see nowhere else, perhaps never see again!"

Had Father Time meant it to sound like a threat? He pushed a lever, and the sub jolted forwards. Surprised, Mikey grabbed at the bolted seat in front. Angus skidded across the polished wooden floor. He glided with an air of smugness about him. Not paying attention, a cactus appeared out of thin air, and Angus collided with it. He yelped and darted around the sub.

"Never mess with me. I can and will get you back. Don't think I didn't see you urinate behind the door; I might be old Angus, but I'm not senile!"

Angus lay in the corner sulking.

They descended deeper, and light from the surface faded. Fish and creatures, he hadn't seen before moved over and under the submarine. Some twirled around, some swam alongside curiously. When the light faded, he pressed a few switches and pulled another lever. A bright light illuminated the bottom of the lake. More strange creatures dodged around; and avoided the light. Father Time winced. Far in the distance, a gigantic creature with teeth and tentacles at least ten times the size of them moved towards the sub. Its eye menacingly reflected green and red.

"This is a creature that normally sits in hibernation half the year. They have disturbed it. While it isn't bad, it gets a little curious. That could mean it swallows us whole."

The submarine engine stopped, and it floated down to the floor with a thud. Metal scraped, and an eye peered through the cockpit, surveying inside. Mikey froze, he'd never seen such an immense creature, sure if he moved, they would die. The sub shook, and Angus flew into Mikey, who grabbed him and held onto the chair for dear life. Had it detected them? The shaking continued and the pressure in the sub built substantially. The sides crushed inwards. Father Time looked terrified; Mikey was sure this was it, how it ended for him.

"Goodbye, I'd love to say it's been a pleasure…"

A loud claxon sounded from above. Bright red flares hit the creature square in its eye. It flailed and dropped them, giving chase. Someone had saved them from a certain demise.

The engine whirred into life and the lights flicked on. The submarine groaned and the crushed sides popped outwards. He hadn't expected to go on an underwater adventure, yet alone face one of the biggest creatures he'd seen. What else was down here?

"What the hell was that?"

"An Octolax. A strong creature that normally minds its own business. They sleep for nine months of the year and are seldom active. I guess our black-eyed friends stirred up more than a few tempers when leaving for Earth."

He thought it looked like an angry octopus, with bigger tentacles.

"How come it let go?"

"The city guard chased it, or rather it chased them. She's obviously angry about the flairs."

"Onwards we go. Sit tight, we have a while yet, may as well get comfortable."

They travelled through the darkness in silence. It was only Angus who broke it with a yawn before he fell asleep. The lake floor beneath them sloped down until it dropped off altogether. Father Time switched off autopilot and manoeuvred the submarine further down in circles. In the distance below, bright lights flickered.

"How did a city end up here?"

"What I'd give to be young and innocent. To be full of curiosity would fill me with joy."

Mikey allowed him to ramble.

"There's a vast city, much bigger than any on the surface. It's the capital of Majjika, and while one of the hardest to reach, it's well worth a visit. It's full of creatures from mere-people to crab-men, fish-elks to seahorses and sea gnomes, a wonderful place with thousands of residents. It's ruled by the self-appointed Mayor Fredrik Seal. Yes, his surname is funny, but don't mistake his last name for humour, he is cunning."

"He became mayor with a name like that?"

"Take heed. He dislikes humour around his name and is renowned for locking people away for sneezing out of turn. Understand, he's involved with all that goes on. He'll know we are here, and it wouldn't surprise me if we're met by a welcome party. Stay with me and let me talk if that happens, okay?"

He diverted his attention back to the window, looking worried as he placed the submarine into autopilot.

Lost in silence for a few minutes as he pondered over information, Mikey had another question pop into his head, a question he'd never had answered before.

"You knew my grandfather, didn't you?"

He nodded, and Mikey assumed he could continue.

"According to my dad, he left his family. It ruined my grandma. He said they had to put her in a mental hospital. Did that make my granddad bad?"

"He wasn't bad, and he didn't leave your family. He sacrificed what remained of his life force, to save everyone, well everyone on Earth. He was a great reaper, fair and rational, unlike your uncle Victor. So you know, your grandmother wasn't crazy, nor was, rather is, your uncle Victor."

Father Time made the familiar err noise again.

"What's wrong,"

"I may have forgotten how to access the city. If I remember correctly, you pass the bubble barrier and get escorted in by city security, it's getting past the bubble that confuses me!"

Mikey poked at every button, but it was no good. The submarine collided with the barrier and ended up half in, half out. Stuck and unable to move, Father Time killed the engine and scratched his head. Mikey about to suggest another idea caught sight of some objects in the distance that looked like large oxygen bubbles with engines. They slowly approached the sub.

"Don't worry, this is normal, I've got to speak to the guard through the bubble mic."

"Unidentified object, please state the nature of your visit to Majji, you have tried to pass the barrier without prior permission being granted!"

"This is Father Time; I request access to Majji to recharge and to get my friend some food and rest."

There was a brief pause before they broadcast a reply.

"We have granted you conditional access to Majji. Please follow your escort to your allocated dock location. Please sign your guest in with city relations, thank you and good day!"

Father Time suggested he strap Angus down and then himself. He went to ask why, but the escort vehicle attached chains to the sub. The vehicle shot forward, pulling the sub free from the barrier. As soon as they were through, the chains released, and the sub plummeted. The barrier kept the water out and the sub dropped through the air. He pressed buttons, but it picked up more speed, approaching the ground fast.

"Err, this is normal, right?!"

"Not really."

A sail shot from the back of the sub, causing it to spin. Mikey pulled a lever and two more sails popped out of the sides. They levelled off and its descent slowed. Father Time looked less worried and grabbed at the steering column, pushing it forwards to follow the escort vehicle waiting ahead.

"All part of the master plan; thought I'd have a little fun. Sit back and enjoy the trip. This city is breath-taking!"

13.

On the deck, a mishmash of buildings were visible across the horizon. He thought this place looked like Manhattan. To the right, an open top tour bus trundled its way down the street. He doubled back when realising the bus bounced up and down and noticed the six giant sea horses. A small speaker blared the inaudible voice of the guide, quite typical of arranged tours back home. A speaker near Mikey groaned and the booming voice of Father Time floated through.

"Note the seahorses. They are a special breed exclusive to the city of Majji. They breathe both through a gill system and through the conventional lungs we have. On land they bob up and down and that's why the tour bus looks uncomfortable."

"I thought sea horses only lived in the sea?"

"When will you learn not every name is related to the area the creatures live, my goodness, what do the teachers, teach back home?"

"I didn't hang around lessons long enough to pay attention."

"If you look to your immediate left, you will see the Fishafella convention centre. Those flags represent each one of Majjika's known relations."

"Known relations?"

"We have business relationships with other worlds, the green one relates to Pretoria, the red one Fataportas and so on.

We import a very important substance from Pretoria named Crystalis, it is our native currency."

A tall building with a globe in front changed colours, flashing excitedly.

"Here we have the Planet Majjiwood building, it has a restaurant serving Majji cuisine and has a museum with memorabilia related to Majjiwood, our very own star-studded movie land."

"But you don't have televisions that I can see?"

"Televisions? We don't need them, we have an on-demand streaming service which we can bring up anywhere via, you guessed it, magic."

A large snake hologram popped out from the building and flew over the top deck. He ducked instinctively. It looked real.

"To the right, note another large skyscraper. This one is the bank of Majji. Here we withdraw and deposit our national currency."

The sub came to a stop to allow a group of elves to cross. They looked a little worse for wear, piling into a two storied building.

"This is one of the most popular pubs in Majjika, The Wailing Merman. I frequented many times. Wonderful place full of fantastic, well usually fantastic atmosphere."

A chair smashed through a window as a bar fight erupted. The sub carried on as the light changed to green.

"You use a traffic light system here?"

"When you have a city full of residents, you need it, believe me. Notice the street vendor on the left?"

"Which one?"

"The one with the pointy blue hat?"

"I can see it, what about it?"

"He creates some of the finest chocolates in all of Majjika. He has so far refused buy outs from Madbury, Lindoff and Westle, three enormous companies."

At another set of lights whilst they waited, he noted a sign. A strange looking woman with thick spectacles looked at him from a tiny window. Underneath her, a plaque read.

'Physic to the stars, Mystic Mel. Have your palm, wing or foot read here,'.

"We are now on forty fish street, the Broadway of Majjika. Here we have shows galore. Over fourteen theatres preside here. One is never bored in Majji."

Outside one of the larger theatres, a small news stand had a little elf in oversized clothing and a flat cap sitting on a highchair. Every now and again he blurted out.

"Read all about it, the FIB strike again in their best sting yet."

"Who is the FIB?"

"The fish-men in black. A very secretive organisation who works only for Mayor Seal. If you spot an official looking suited and booted fish, well man, it means the Mayor is around, or you're in trouble."

A creature with six arms crossed over another busy crossing, holding many leads.

"That woman has pet millipedes?"

"Speak into the microphone and don't mumble."

"I said, she has millipedes as pets?"

"Yes, giant millipedes. They are popular here. Too many legs for my liking."

A creature riding one of the giant sea horses bounded by and shouted out of a microphone.

"Vote Mayor Fredrik Seal in the upcoming election. He is

the only choice!"

"As broadcasted, the election is coming up, I'm hoping the opposition gets a sniff this time."

"I don't understand politics, never did."

"You don't understand the polish?"

"No Father Time, politics. This microphone is a little dodgy, you sound like an alien."

"If you look in front, you can see the statue of Malto the dog. There was an awful outbreak of Miles disease in nineteen twenty-five. He carried the cure to over one thousand residents, saving their lives. For that they immortalised him as a statue. Some speculate he still roams the park at night, helping lost residents find their way out, others say he is the statue."

"I'd run a mile if a statue of a dog came to life and approached me anywhere!"

"If you look to your immediate left, you'll see the Lavincii musical clock, built in nineteen sixty-five, a personal favourite of mine."

"You like a clock; I'd never have guessed."

"Don't get cheeky with me, Mr Birt."

"You sound like my head teacher, well old one."

"Well as I was going to say before you interrupted, this clock plays twinkle, twinkle, little star and parades various figures."

The chime rang out on the clock and the music started. One by one tiny figures moved to the front, bowed, and moved back behind a door. Father Time appeared, followed by Mother Nature and a hooded cloaked figure.

"You have a figure of yourself on a clock, that's vain. The funny thing is, it's taller than you…"

"Excuse me!"

"What I mean to say, is they have immortalised your likeness?"

"I suppose they have. Did you catch the person in the cloak?"

"Yes, who is he?"

"That is your grandfather, well not that you can see, as the cloak covers his face, but trust me, it's Charles. I would suggest you re-join me in the cockpit please, I think the microphone is on the fritz."

He re-joined Father Time and Angus, who snored away. The park hosted a festival with thousands of creatures in attendance. In the middle a castle took centre stage, guarded by a giant statue with long wispy hair and a beard. He recognised this creature as a merman. Behind, a lake stretched out, its shoreline resembled that of a sandy beach. He rubbed his eyes when out popped two eight-foot fishes, who sprouted limbs and walked away hand in hand.

"That's Mr and Mrs Pisces; they own the lake, they are, Fishple."

"Fishple, what are they?"

"A most curious creature able to grow limbs on land and lose them in water."

Mikey thought Mrs Pisces was quite beautiful. Her perfectly symmetrical scales glistened in the light.

"Pisces, as in the star sign?"

"Yes. As a point of interest, What's your star sign?"

"I think I'm a Virgo, but it's rubbish."

"Not as much as you think. The constellations are portraits formed from stars by the great artist 'Banksea'. Yes, I know you have one in your world, spelled different, they aren't the same person."

The image of some cosmic street artist arranging the stars was hard to get his head around. The submarine slowed to a crawl as it approached the dock. With a splash, they landed in the water at pier number seven. A group of gnomes similar to the garden variety, lazily threw a mooring rope around and pulled them in. Their skin had a greenish hue, and they had webbed hands and feet. The hatch of the submarine twisted open, and they heaved Angus up. The unmistakable scent of a seashore greeted them as they disembarked. Surprised by the sway, Mikey nearly lost balance and fell into the water. Father Time looked pale. The travel hadn't agreed with him.

"Is everything okay, you don't look, ouch!"

He felt a prod and turned to see one creature; its hand held out. Mikey shrugged and shook it. The gnome tutted and spat into his palm. Father Time stepped in, yelling through the noise.

"Terribly sorry, my friend is new to Majji. Take extra as my way of apology. He meant no offence, my good gnome!"

From his pocket he withdrew an amount of small crystals, handing them to the gnome. It growled and walked to the next vessel, ready to dock.

"Best not annoy the sea-gnomes, they work for little, relying on tips to boost income. Crystalis don't grow on trees!"

Mikey understood, glad Father Time came along to help adjust in Majjika.

"Majji is massive and over a hundred miles across. We must rest up, then resume at dawn."

Angus spun on the spot and with a splash, landed in the water. He swam in circles in search for something.

"It's not another dog, you idiot, it's your reflection!"

Mikey grabbed Angus's collar and pulled him out. In return, he shook water everywhere.

"Angus, you are the sworn protector of the Veil, and I know you have training to show restraint when dog-like situations arise. Behave or we'll go without you!"

Angus shook the last of the water from his fur and sat.

"This isn't good, I expected a welcome party, not the Mayor himself. No questions, let me talk!"

A large entourage made their way over. Similar creatures to Mr and Mrs Pisces, they sported black suits and sunglasses. In the middle a portly half-man, half seal, slithered forwards. One of the entourages spoke into his earpiece, giving the all clear. The Mayor approached Father Time.

"Mr Time, what brings you too Majji? Holiday, relaxation, perhaps a spot of gambling? It's strange you arrived differently to your, usual mode of transportation?"

Father Time rubbed his hands through his hair.

"Mr Mayor, if you address me by title, it is Dr Time. My reason for visiting is my own. Our intention is to rest and be on our way."

"I see you've a guest, with a magical artefact. One which belonged to Victor Birt. Who's the boy, Dr Time?"

"This is Victor's grandson, Michael, I mean, nephew. I'm sure you're aware the black-eyed kids vacated Majjika and they now terrorise Earth."

The Mayor cackled.

"It's a God send. If they destroy someone else's world, what a shame, bon voyage, I say!"

"You cannot abandon Earth. If they grab the artefacts left in the human world, then we will be powerless to stop them, I implore you see reason!"

The Mayor dumbfounded by the verbal attack pondered.

A malicious grin spread across his face.

"I've said before, hold your tongue with me! You think Majjika gives two hoots about the world outside of our own, you're deluded. Humans destroy all they touch; they have met their match!"

Father Time opened his mouth, but words failed him. Mikey wouldn't allow this with too much at stake.

"Fredrik Seal, your attitude stinks! You have a beautiful city and I've met some wonderful beings in this world. There's plenty of good on Earth, and that's worth saving, regardless of your opinion!"

The Mayor turned crimson and his bushy eyebrows covered his face.

"Insolent little half-breed how dare you address Mayor Fredrick Elijah Seal without my title. You aren't home now; you'll be punished for your insolence!"

"I'd rather be a half-breed than have a last name like yours. You ugly, pathetic little man, bullying people because you're a mayor!"

Father Time squeaked as suits wrestled them to the ground. Angus howled, biting at anyone he could, but it was no good. They restrained and muzzled him. Mikey's head pressed hard against the wooden floor so he could only see the bottom half of the mayor.

"Think your brief outburst was funny? Take them to the dungeons, but be quiet about it, you'll wake my constituents!"

"He didn't mean it, let's start again, please, we have important information to share!"

A loud crack pierced the air and Father Time fell silent. Mikey struggled and before he could move an inch, one of the entourages whacked him across the head, rendering him unconscious.

14.

Between the voices and squeak of wheels, it was a wonder no one noticed the commotion. Mikey drifted in-between consciousness, making out several silhouettes. Two pulled the cart that carried them. A cloth hid them from view. The Fishman closest to Mikey's side spoke. It seemed the Mayor's instructions to be quiet fell on deaf ears.

"Look at this disgusting human, how's that normal? No thanks, rather be part sea-gnome!"

The others laughed; they disliked humans. The cart halted in a lit passageway.

"Mayor wants to store some goods, let them ferment a bit, if you know what I mean!"

The guard pulled out his key chain, placed one into the lock, and opened the large iron gate in-wards. The cart moved again, and Mikey drifted out of consciousness.

A hushed voice called out as Eva appeared. She reached out to him.

"Michael, hello, I need you!"

He reached out, and she moved toward him, hair blowing in the light breeze. He stroked her face. Recoiling in disgust, she grabbed a jug and threw the contents over him.

"Michael Birt, what in the name of time are you doing, wake up! Under no circumstances, do you touch me!"

He woke with Father Time stood over, less than

impressed!

"I thought you were Eva!"

Mikey took in the damp stone room with its iron door. A grate allowed a minuscule amount of light, and a lingering stench offended his nostrils.

"Listen for the guard, there's one way out. I have little energy, but I must try."

"How do we get out?"

"The master watch. I'll summon and transform it into another object, then we can escape!"

"What's the worst that can happen?"

"I spontaneously combust, or the world folds in on itself."

He peered through the keyhole, across the long empty corridor, with the odd whimper coming from Angus beyond.

Father Time positioned himself under the grate, lifting his arms.

'I command the master watch return to me!'

He repeated, but nothing appeared.

"I mustn't have the energy."

Mikey repeated the words.

A scuttle and squeak above revealed a small mouse which dropped into the room. It fled to the corner and briefly shone yellow. They both dived, and it flitted between hands and shot towards a gap which they covered. As the mouse back tracked Father Time cupped it.

"There you are old friend! I asked for a rat, close enough."

It changed to the pocket watch, which he wiped against his suit carefully. Opening the cover, he pushed a button and disappeared, leaving him alone.

"Father Time!"

Had he been too weak and vanished? Mikey pushed the

door, but it wouldn't budge. Angus barked as a voice shouted.

"Shush boy, you'll get us caught!"

A pitter patter of feet bounded down the corridor. Through the gap, Angus sniffed. Father Time followed and pulled a set of keys from his pocket, trying each one in the lock. The door creaked open.

"We don't have long. The guard will realise the keys have gone!"

He followed Father Time down the well-lit corridor. If someone came, they'd have nowhere to hide.

"No matter what happens, this is bigger than us. I will provide a distraction if needed. Find Eva and Victor, stop those kids before it's too late. There's something you should know about her, she's a…"

A claxon noise interrupted, and they marched up the passage to the main courtyard. Greeted by the chant of thousands, demanding a leadership change, it seemed politics in Majjika and Earth were the same, corrupted. The courtyard extended to reveal a veranda set above. In the middle-stood Mayor Seal, who greeted the crowd.

"People of Majji. In this most difficult of times, it is crucial we have strong leadership. I Mayor Fredrik Elijah Seal promise to rule with a firm hand until such a time you all learn to follow the rules!"

He clicked his fingers and the courtyard gates lowered. Father Time ushered Mikey under one before it slammed shut. The jeers changed to screams, and a relative of the Easter Bunny jumped forwards.

"He's a monster, everyone's doomed, please help!"

Father Time pulled the gate, it wouldn't budge. Already weakened, he grabbed the master watch, which transformed into a key. Even if it was the only gate open, at least it gave a chance of escape. The resulting stampede almost took Angus, who ducked and skidded to Mikey. They pressed against the wall, waiting as everyone passed, before locking the gate. Hopefully it would slow down the fish-men.

"We board the ship at the docks; I have no energy and need rest. It will layover at Ferry Wood island, then we continue by sub, or the ship once refuelled."

They waited to board, it's red and white sails floated lazily, as it bobbed side to side. A portly merman accosted them in the line.

"Advanced tickets only!"

"We don't have tickets; can't we purchase them?"

"We're at capacity, come back tomorrow!"

He pulled down the hatch, locking it into place.

"Marcell, please, there must be space? How many times have I got you out of trouble!"

Marcell signalled to the luggage loader on the left. Father Time pushed past the crowd with Mikey in tow. He apologised as they made their way through.

"Excuse me, mate."

Atop the luggage bridge, Marcell distracted the handler, pointing which direction to head in. They boarded before the hatch closed for departure, sneaking into the corridor that linked the luggage section to the wooden staircase of the floor above. It led to a decorated hallway with pictures of different animals and creatures. One picture of a large woman, on closer inspection, revealed her eyes were black, and her hands clawed. She perched on top of a rock in rough seas in front of a lighthouse. A caption read.

'Lobwom, Protector of the lighthouse, walker of the

Seabed.'

Mikey opened a black door with a golden handle to reveal a prettier, wider staircase, this one full of the passengers headed to the living quarters above. The inhabitants stepped on a ring, and a small disc moved them to the decks above. It happened so quickly he pondered how they stayed on.

"Magic."

Father Time always knew his thoughts. Maybe he questioned the obvious?

"The green ring goes up, the yellow down. When you get on, request the floor you wish in Majjikan, it will take you there."

Mikey didn't know Majjikan or the floor he needed. Father Time stepped forwards.

"Uno."

The disc appeared, and he vanished. Mikey stepped on the ring with Angus, took a deep breath and muttered.

"Uno."

A strange force held his feet down and Angus looked at his paws, confused. The disc underneath sent them upwards and in the seconds that passed he counted decks. The ship had thirty. They arrived at the correct floor, confirmed by a metal plaque at the side that read 'Uno.' He spotted Father Time conversing with a creature with a tail and a patch over his left eye. His ears poked through his hat. Father Time spotted him and excused himself.

"How did you find the lifts?"

"Scary and fast!"

"I find them pleasant, much quicker than on Earth. Fun fact, they haven't broken down in two hundred years!"

"Who's the creature?"

"He's a Pirat, born to the waters of Majjika, knows them better than anyone."

"Did you say pirate?"

"No Pirat. Though his ancestors were seen on Earth a few hundred years ago, from a distance they appeared human like. They got a bad name and all things sinister are associated with pirates."

The decor had a modern twist, but signs of an ageing ship were present. Its windows looked dirty and the seals holding them in place perished. The lights had a fine layer of dust, and the wooden support beams had hairline cracks around the edges. The ship made no sense. Then again, this was Majjika. Father Time returned with two full pitchers of Pilichee and passed one across.

"To a drama-free voyage, may it go forwards with ease!"

Mikey toasted, though Eva sat on his mind. Until they found her, he wouldn't be able to rest.

"We don't have a cabin, there is however a communal area to unwind. Perhaps you might rest there?"

Though the Veil would prohibit sleep, he took the chance to rest his eyes. Headed to the communal area, he agreed to meet Father Time when they docked on Ferry Wood island. Angus followed.

15.

Sometime later, Father Time confirmed they'd docked. The captain announced a stopover while they refuelled, suggesting everyone see the island. Wanting to stretch after being cramped in a cot, Mikey took the opportunity. They passed Marcell, who handed them three ticket stubs. The temperature of the island seemed hotter than the city region they came from. It seemed at some point; the ship ascended through the water and landed on the surface. Palm trees lined the streets, and between every other sat a banana plant.

"Are they banana plants and palm trees?"

"Both native here and introduced to Earth when the orangutans migrated. They lost the ability to speak."

"Why take the palm trees to Earth?"

"Palm was a favourite food of the Oranga tribesmen when they emigrated."

The delicious aroma of food caught their attention. They located the source, a small hut shaped like a coconut with its small windows steamed up, and a chimney poked out the top. Through the front door a small elf greeted them in a pointy hat, his accent reminiscent of the Caribbean.

"Whadup ma man, you here for grub? We got da best palm stew this side of Majjika. We got banana and palm fritter, palm juice, Pilichee and palm juice, my personal favourite and much more my man!"

Mikey decided on stew, made with palm sugar and a secret blend of five spices. Delicious, it melted in his mouth.

Next up he chose the banana and palm fritter, a dessert deep fried in batter. It tasted fantastic. He washed it down with Pilichee and palm juice, remembering he had no way to pay for it. Father Time rolled his eyes and pulled out some Crystalis to pay the elf. Mikey thanked him and they made their way out.

"If creatures here need not eat, why do they serve food?"

"Do you eat because you are hungry, or because you enjoy it?"

"Both, I guess. I eat chocolate, even when I'm not hungry. Love the stuff."

"Majjika might not need food, but we love to try new things. It's a hobby for some."

They took in the sights and sounds, stopping near a billboard of a green island and rainbow. Angus cocked his leg but jumped back when a voice echoed.

"Oi stinky great brute, get your leg off mi post!"

They watched a small ginger haired man in a green suit climb out, brushing himself off.

"Oi you there, this your dumb mutt."

"Don't call Angus stupid?"

"Or else wot? This boy and dog with you?"

"Yes Amos, they are."

"Get that mutt from mi island or kiss your luck goodbye."

"What you gonna do?"

The small man launched himself at Mikey, flailing his fists in the air.

"A wee bit of help boys."

Several others jumped from the billboard surrounding

him.

"Michael, please apologise!"

"Why should I apologise! Fine, sorry!"

"Apologise like you mean it, that was not good enough!"

"I'm sorry."

Amos stepped back, putting his arms down.

"That's enough boys, I think he's learnt his lesson."

"Don't know what I did wrong?"

"You made fun of me! I mean the ignorance of it; I don't appreciate arrogance. Next time apologise. Remember, we're Leprechauns, we can throw bad luck your way, or worse."

Amos beckoned to the others, and they climbed back through the billboard. A little hand popped out and gave Mikey the finger. He blinked, and it vanished.

"Come on, I'd suggest trying to avoid trouble, if that's not too difficult!"

At a crossroads, they arrived at an old brick building with a thatched straw roof. A swaying sign above the door read 'Dog Inn.'

Mikey erupted in laughter, stifling it with his hand.

"What's funny?"

"It's called Dog Inn, I mean if they knew what I do, they'd call it another name. Can't say why it's rude!"

Father Time pressed to the entrance, opened the door and slammed it.

When he couldn't laugh anymore, he picked himself up off the ground. Amazed how many people the inn could fit inside, he looked around.

Bars lined the walls with many types of drinks, either mixed with Pilichee in a crazy concoction, or without the native drink of Majjika. Father Time sat, tankard in hand.

Parched, he strolled over. Father Time handed one to him before he could ask and held his up, downing it in one. He called the barman and ordered another.

Mikey wondered if it was more than Pilichee. His eyes rolled back and out of character, he barked.

"Mickey, Mikey, Michael. Let's stay the night and set off in the hic, morning? There's always another ship!"

He had to convince an inebriated Father Time to stop drinking.

"Get a move on, the ship will leave without us. You've drunk enough!"

Father Time swung on the stool, lost his balance and smiled.

"Relax, I'll be right as rain in a moment. The unfortunate t-t-thing about me, alcohol kicks in for a minute, then the effects wear off!"

By the end of the sentence he'd sobered, paid the tab and they exited. Past the coconut hut and back down to the pier, they waited to re-board. A distinct voice sounded in the background. Mayor Fredrik Seal had followed them, this time with no entourage.

Father Time hugged and exchanged jokes with him. Yesterday he'd imprisoned them.

"Don't panic, this is Fredrik Seal's brother Trent, an identical triplet. He's a spoken critic of his family, believe me he hates his brother more than we do."

Trent pulled him in for a bear hug.

"It's good to meet Victor's nephew, he's a cool cucumber. Sorry if my brother upset you, he's a moron, that's my family, come to think of it!"

Mikey didn't appreciate being manhandled but held out

his hand to shake.

"Handshakes are for strangers; I know all about your family and that Veil."

They bid farewell to Trent, who hugged Father Time once more and walked away.

"I thought we were done for; you never mentioned the mayor had brothers!"

"There are many things I know. Perhaps I should have mentioned that was not Fredrik, then again I thought you deserved to sweat it out for the trouble you caused earlier!"

They boarded, finding seats in a corner of the Pilichee cafe.

The ship docked with a slight bump after two attempts because of rough water. The crew set the moorings for disembarkation. Passengers made their way off and the captain and crew bade farewell, as accustomed in all forms of major transport. Glad to be off the ship, Father Time hummed a melody which he recognised. They took care to cross over the pier towards the exit, strolling past another docked ship. A familiar voice sounded from its top deck.

"Yoo hoo Father Time, up here!"

"It's Mother Nature, wonder why she's travelled this way."

"It's that wretched woman. We need to escape before she gets off the, too late!"

She barged through the crowd at such a pace, Mikey wondered why she needed a walking cane. On approach, a faint glow of rouge appeared on her cheeks. She clearly had a crush on Father Time.

"Don't you dare mutter a word, I'm past human constructs!"

"That's what she said, funnily enough!"

"Hello Mikey, nice to see you again."

"Dear woman, we are in a terrible rush, can't stop to chit chat. Got to rescue that girl and all."

"Well, perhaps it would be quicker if you let me help you!"

"We may need her help, Father Time, the more the merrier!"

"Absolutely not, no way, she would slow us down. I insist we continue without her!"

"Unless you really can help, we've got to go."

"I like that Eva girl. I feel partly responsible. Let me help you find her."

"Fine, but you better not slow us down!"

He strolled behind; unsure they would get on. It surprised him when Father Time responded well to a topic of conversation.

"I think you might be right."

"It's the truth," said Mother Nature. "Creatures have been far more relaxed since they left."

"Like I said, time will tell. The black-eyed kids have done this before, remember?"

"How could I forget, how could anyone?"

"We won once before; I suppose we'll do it again."

"This is different, we had Charles, this time we have, inexperience."

"By inexperience, you mean me. Speaking of inexperience, you seem to like each other?"

Father Time slipped on a slimy boulder, falling flat on his bottom.

"Ouch! Don't be stupid, we are both past such human

construct. Isn't that right, Mother Nature?"

"Like Father said, he is, I mean, we are past such human constructs, simply two individuals aware of each other!"

"You act in a way that tells me otherwise. He's stubborn and you're in denial, you're not sure how to read each other, are you?"

They replied in unison.

"Shut up, mind your own business!"

He wondered about all the girls who'd liked him and how many he ignored. Father Time stopped to converse with someone in a cloak.

"Why you galloping around with a reaper? Thought you'd know better than to 'ang with them?"

"Come now, Coop," responded Mother Nature. "Don't judge others, we are helping Mikey find Eva, have you seen her on your travels?"

"It was hard not to on account of her breaking one of my tables, he broke the other. Ever 'erd of landing? I enjoyed being the only human 'ere, on account of my parents sodding off and leaving me to be raised by elves. Now there's three of us, everyone will talk they will!"

"Cooper, Michael's not all human, he's a reaper. Eva is a, well, she's the girl we need to rescue!"

"I sense I've outstayed my welcome with this conversation, I bid good day sirs and miss."

Father Time and Mother Nature walked ahead and continued in quiet conversation. They looked back now and then.

"I know you're talking about me; I've heard my name a few times. What is it you won't tell me?"

Neither would look him in the eye.

"You're yet to understand," said Father Time. "Once we find Eva, make sure she gets home. Under no circumstances can you be together. It is for the greater good!"

"What's so much of a secret you can't tell me? I should know all you do; we are trying to rescue Eva after all!"

"There are things I cannot discuss. Victor should be the one to explain, if you can rescue him."

"I think I deserve an answer to why I can't be with a girl I've fallen for!"

"I promise when it's time to talk, we will," said Mother Nature. "We must concentrate on getting you both back home!"

"Fine, if you treat me like a child, I've nothing to say!"

They crossed a hilltop and passed a sign to the nearest village. The distinct smell of burnt wood hit their nostrils. In the distance, a fire raged. Father Time sprinted as fast as his legs would carry him.

"You two stay here!"

They followed towards the fire, not ready for what they were to find.

16.

Out of breath and amazed Mother Nature kept up, he speculated it wasn't on her own steam. She patted her cane affectionately, pressing it into the ground to lean. He caught its finer details, a green wooden cane with a simple twist in the middle and an ornate handle curved around, finished by a leather cover. They paused at a rope bridge which joined the village to the wider province. Its inter-weaved structure supported various wooden planks that had seen better days. As it was the only path across, they carefully crossed as it flailed at the slightest touch. On the other side, Father Time retched. He picked himself up and examined the locals attempts to put out the fire. Mikey snatched a wooden pail by its iron handle and made his way to the river. When the bucket filled, he dashed to a cottage and hurled the contents over its straw roof.

"You two, take a bucket and help?"

"There aren't enough, I can't move much, I'm half your height."

"Will you please do something!"

Mother Nature lifted her cane, her words inaudible because of the commotion. The sky churned, developing thick shadowy clouds. Rain poured and in minutes they suppressed the fires. A giant hare creature bound across.

"Thank you. It was one of those damn goblins. It used a torch to set fire to the village. My wife was inside when it took place, I'd nipped to the tavern for refreshment."

A terrible wail pierced the smoky air and Mikey fell to his knees, disorientated. The air became icy cool, and his heart tugged. The wail increased until he thought his heart shattered and then reduced to a sob. Through the smoke, the Easter Bunny arrived, bringing a small bunny. She pleaded for it to wake, but it remained soft and lifeless.

"Father Time, Mother Nature, our little Hoppy's hurt. Please save him, I beg of you?!"

Both looked disoriented, Father Time moved to Mikey's side trying to lift him.

"It is time. The pain now won't ever escape you. There is nothing I can do; you must bring him to his sunny place."

Uncontrollable tears dropped from his face and he swayed his head.

"What am I supposed to do? He's only a small bunny. I don't want to reap him. Why me?"

"It's who you are. You are from a line of reapers. You will not hurt him; but move him to the next life. Hoppy is in trouble, please help."

He stood with support from Father Time, stepping toward the Easter Bunny,

"Miss Bunny, I can't bring him back. I think I can take away the pain, help stop the suffering."

Distraught, the Easter Bunny, looked at her brother. Tears raced down her cheek, and she nodded, placing Hoppy gently on the ground. Badly burned and covered in blood, he lay lifeless. Mikey placed his hand gently onto Hoppy and the world around transformed into the village before the fire. Truly a stunning village, everyone moved along with business. The lifeless body of Hoppy disappeared.

"Hoppy, I'm a family friend, come out please, I won't hurt you."

A door handle rattled and out came Hoppy with a cheeky smile.

"Hi, it's nice to meet you!"

"Hi. I, where, are we?"

"Littlewood village, the happiest village around!"

He seemed unfazed around a reaper.

"I have news with no straightforward way to deliver it."

"Did my sister send you to play with me, I've been lonely without her, where is she?"

Mikey's heart broke, he didn't understand.

"Your sister sent me, but not to play, please come with me."

"Where are we going?"

"Where's your cheerful place?"

"With my mum, dad and sister!"

"Where's your parents?"

"They're in the house sill…"

He stopped short of what he wanted to say. The smile vanished, and he bent in agony.

"Sorry."

He knelt, placing both hands-on Hoppy's shoulder. Words he didn't recognise left his mouth.

"Ego autem te ad locum beatus, vive feliciter amicus."

Words played around his head in English, but he spoke them out in Latin. Hoppy breathed one last breath, smiled, then disappeared. The village around Mikey blurred, and the buildings changed to burnt out husks. The Easter Bunny cradled her brother, tears falling down her swollen face. His time had ended and the best they could do was stop the suffering. What kind of power was that? A voice spoke from behind.

"Tell sis I see mama and papa. I'm in a much better place. Explain we'll be together again, one day. She won't believe it, say I cracked the golden egg, and it flooded the house with chocolate."

Hoppy faded, and a weight lifted. He repeated what Hoppy said and her tears stopped.

"Our Hoppy is okay?"

"Yes, he's with your parents now. He had a cheeky smile, said sorry about the crack."

"I wondered how it happened, oh how I'll miss him. Hoppy was the only family left."

"I didn't know, I'm sorry."

"I'll see him again. I have to lay him to rest with my parents."

"Let me help, It's the least I can do?"

"I need to do this alone."

She mouthed a thank you, then hopped off in the distance to bury her brother with her family. Mikey felt a pair of arms steer him toward a bench.

"I must sit; the old legs aren't quite what they used to be dear," said Mother Nature, "are you okay?"

"I don't think so. The best I can do is end the suffering?"

"I remember when Victor first reaped a soul, it brought sadness to him and he couldn't process how life never ends, it's a cycle."

"I didn't ask for this job."

"Sometimes those who don't want the job are best placed to do it?"

"I hope we can get him back, my uncle, I mean."

"He spoke of you, wanted to meet you earlier, but your father was distant and never gave Victor that chance to be part of your life. He is alive, I feel it."

"I will find him, I promise!"

"That's the spirit, let that spare you on. Let's help clean up, it's the least we can do."

Joining the villagers, they stacked and chopped wood, cleared the cobblestone pathway and salvaged what they could. Mother Nature pointed at burnt husks of trees and encouraged them to grow. She pointed at two ash trees and they overlapped to form a cross, carving into the bark, 'RIP Hoppy, Brother and friend to all.' A commotion up near the bridge erupted.

"Help, the fire goblin wants to burn our bridge to the ground!"

This creature cost Hoppy his life, caused the Easter Bunny more pain and terrorised an entire village. Mikey and Angus sprinted before anyone could react. The goblin failed to light a torch and got tackled to the ground.

"You killed an innocent bunny, I had to reap him, you monster, why?!"

The goblin looked up, a big grin on his face.

"Orders, you think I give two hoots about the village?"

"Why this village!?"

"Knew it was on your path and it would get your attention! They are always watching!"

"Who's watching, tell me or I swear!"

"If you hurt the goblin," said Father Time, panting, "you'll be no better. Please think this through!"

"He killed Hoppy, what did he do to deserve that?!"

The goblin laughed.

"I told you, wasn't about the village or villagers, it's your attention they wanted. They watch you!"

"You're dead for this!"

"I don't care, the job's done! I don't feel great, anyhow."

"Who sent you, you horrible creature!"

The goblin, gurgled.

"I have to tell you, closer, I need to whisper."

He had his ear an inch from the goblin's mouth.

"The... black... eyed..."

The goblin's eyes went black and a cruel malice spread across its face.

"Ooh, big scary reaper, did we get your attention?!"

"Yeah, I swear I'll kill you all. Where is my uncle!"

"When you get back to Earth, bring us the Veil, or your uncle gets it!"

"No chance, I know what you'd do with it. My uncle gave it to me to stop you!"

"If you care for his life, you'll give it to us. We are everywhere and see all!"

"Where do I find you?!"

"We will find you, reaper, ha, ha, ha!"

The goblin burst into flames. Father Time used all his strength to pull Mikey backwards.

"It knew where my uncle was, I could have found him!"

"They toy with you," said Father Time, "under no circumstances, hand over the Veil. Victor gave it to you for a reason."

"What can I do?!"

"Find Eva, get her home, focus on one mission at a time."

"How can they corrupt like that? Maybe the goblin was innocent?"

"The black-eyed kids corrupted many families; their capabilities have grown."

"Possession, like say a demonic possession?"

"Very much like that. They have found power, but it isn't a complete source. They only possessed the goblin for a short while. That suggests their powers aren't as strong as they could be. We don't know who we can trust, they can corrupt anyone."

"They could corrupt you, Mother Nature, even Fredrik Seal?"

"Mother Nature and I have never had contact with them. We are ourselves to the best of my knowledge. As for Fredrik Seal, it makes sense, they could corrupt him."

"We need to make a move, Eva is on her own," declared Mother Nature, "If they can track us, they must know who we search for."

"If they've already got her, I'll never forgive myself or Victor!"

"Ladies are organised, I'm one hundred percent sure she's fine!"

"Let's hope you're right and we catch up to her," said Mikey, taking to his feet.

17.

Travelling through lengthy fields, they often heard strange noises in the long grasses. Passers-by greeted with a nod, the bow of a hat, one even curtsied. In the middle of one field, Father Time sniffed the air.

"The fragrant scent of Calluna Vulgaris, marvel at the colours!"

This field had mauve coloured flowers with a familiar scent. It brought Mikey back to Scotland.

"Calluna what?"

"Calluna Vulgaris," replied Mother Nature, "known as heather, a plant grandmother cultivated!"

"Well, thank goodness she did," responded Father Time "without it we wouldn't have Pilichee!"

"Pilichee contains heather?"

"It's a key ingredient, one of the few brought from Earth and cultivated. From time to time we borrow."

"I attended a wedding once, staying near fields of this in Scotland. My parents mentioned they brewed a beer with it. I wanted to try, but my dad's religious and doesn't touch the 'devil's juice'. Do you know why my dad turned to religion; did he know about the Veil?"

"No," said Father Time, "only Victor."

"No one believed him?"

"If not for us, he would go crazy with burden," Mother

Nature said.

"I think I understand now. He didn't want me to end up like my father. When he knew me, he didn't want me running off with a girl like my dad?"

Father Time turned away and Mother Nature scratched her ear.

"Yes, that'll be what it was. Look ahead, you might recognise the look of them!"

In the field, rows and rows of golden coloured berries glistened in the light. They looked like strawberries with green stems and yellow leaves. His stomach rumbled, and he grabbed the nearest plant, pulling off a few of the berries. The familiar flavour of strawberry hit his palette, then changed to a salted caramel and butterscotch.

"Dig in, they're delicious!"

Mother Nature looked at Father Time, and he slapped his palm against his forehead.

"Do you grab and eat plants without knowing what they are back home?!"

"I, um, they're golden strawberry's?"

"Similar, but they contain a chemical which, well, they are Laughberries, that'll give you some sign."

A strange sensation built in the pit of his stomach and his face flushed red.

"Erm, Father Time, ha-ha, Father Time, I can't stop myself, this is funny!"

He fell in fits of giggles.

"How many did he eat," said Mother Nature, "remember that poor lady leprechaun, what's her name?"

"Linda Gigglesworth, I remember her well, poor thing!"

"Wait, ha-ha, what happened to, Linda?"

"Well, she erm, wet herself. Yes, leprechauns have toilet needs. The effects lasted a while!"

"You mean, ha-ha, this could go on?"

"The effects last one hour to two days per berry," said Mother Nature, "it depends how your body processes them!"

"How long did Linda feel like this, ha-ha?"

"Father Time, do you remember?"

"Three days, seven hours and thirteen minutes, or thereabouts!"

He choked on saliva, struggling to catch a breath.

"Three days, I can't ha-ha, cope with this for three days!"

"There's a reliever of symptoms named weep leaf," said Mother Nature.

"Ha-ha, weep leaf?!"

"It grows near Laughberry and needs administering in small doses. Too much and you'll cry yourself to death!"

"I'll risk it, ha-ha, please, I'll risk it!"

She stooped and tugged a brown plant, snapping a piece off.

"I know plants, this will be enough. I won't lie, it tastes like salty celery!"

It was better to taste that flavour than laugh himself to death. He opened his mouth, and she shoved it in, resisting the urge to throw up, he chewed and the urge to laugh subsided.

"I'd have eaten the berry's without thought, and wouldn't have got to Eva, thank you!"

"Best err on the side of caution!"

The Laughberries lined the next three fields. The generic green grass fields returned and Mikey rubbed his calve muscles. How much could his legs cope with today?

The fields changed to an almost recognisable plant.

Shaped like love hearts, they produced a sweet floral scent reminiscent of lavender.

"This smells like lavender, but its flowers look like little hearts. What are they?"

Father Time exchanged worried looks with Mother Nature.

"It's the Lovender plant. Breathe in too much of the scent and you become loved up. It won't create false emotions; it brings locked up feelings to the surface."

"I get it, I have feelings for you, but you don't. I realise it's ridiculous, Mother Nature holds a flame for Father Time. You are cute!"

"I'm flattered, but we must remain professional, we are the only ones in our, who am I kidding, you are beautiful! Your hair is Earthy, and you have a most wonderful distinct erm, smell!"

He grabbed at Mother Nature's hand and then at Father Times, dragging them on.

"We need to move, you two can work on your emotions later!"

"I'm glad I met you, Father Time. I know you pretend not to care, and I insist I'm passed such human constructs, but, I love you!"

"You love me?"

"I long to be with you!"

"My dear woman, I feel the same!"

"This plant isn't doing the two of you any favours. I need both your heads in the game, sort your love out after!"

Through the Lovender fields they climbed a hill, descending into a valley. A distinct, consistent rumble sounded ahead of them.

"Is that water I hear?"

Father Time rubbed at his head.

"We are near a river, it's what fills the lake downstream. I don't remember the fields. How did we get here? Oh no!"

The sudden realisation of what happened hit.

"Mother Nature, what I said, it's not that I didn't mean it, but it would be inappropriate for us to act. They need us in both worlds, and we are both busy!"

Mother Nature cleared her throat, wiping tears away from her cheeks.

"I agree, as you say, far too busy. However true the feelings!"

Mikey felt the mediator.

"It's normal to have emotions, but discuss it after we get Eva?"

Mother Nature and Father Time replied.

"Shut up, we don't want to talk about it!"

The river to the left flowed. A footpath ascended, and they followed. At a grey stone bridge that crossed a huge waterfall. It cascaded underneath, and the light reflected off the mist, creating a rainbow. Amos popped his head out, signalled to say, 'I'm watching you' then disappeared. He'd annoyed the wrong creature and wondered if he'd ever let it go. The steep steps leading to the bridge made his legs shake. Mother Nature must have shared his fear.

"Is there no other way? That looks unsafe, you won't get me on it!"

The bridge had seen better days. The mortar between bricks crumbled, and the floor suffered various cracks, some that large you could see light through them.

"It's the bridge, or we leave Eva to fend for herself."

Mother Nature sat on a stump leaning against her cane; Angus sniffed it.

'I won't go over, no way!'

"I didn't request your company; you volunteered your services. Get up or we leave without you!"

"How dare you," responded Mother Nature, "Mikey invited me!"

"Well I didn't, I told him you'd slow us!"

"I volunteered my services, not to cross a broken bridge atop a waterfall!"

"If there's another way, I'm all ears!"

Unable to provide a valid alternative, she headed to the bridge, climbing the stone steps before she could change her mind. Father Time broke into a small run to keep up. At the foot of the bridge they stopped. Able to see the torrent of water underneath, through the cracks it brought home how dangerous it was to cross. He took a deep breath and stepped onto the bridge, taking care to navigate the holes in the floor below. About the halfway mark, things went wrong. The bridge groaned and the already fragile walls crumbled. Mother Nature squeaked and grabbed onto Father Time's arm. Angus bound past and the floor in front of him opened up, sending him into the river. Mikey reached the side of the riverbank, bolting downstream as fast as possible, ignoring the screams behind.

"Angus, hold on, I'll get you out of there!"

He scrambled to a boulder bulging out into the river and grabbed a log, lying flat on his stomach. He placed the log out, hoping Angus would grab it with his jaws. With all his strength, he heaved and pulled Angus close enough to grab his collar. On the boulder, he shook himself off and covered everyone with water.

"Keep a tighter leash on him," said Mother Nature, "you could've drowned, now I'm soaked!"

"Don't start," said Father Time, "he saved Angus!"

"Give it a rest. I did what anyone would, he's my uncle's dog. Let's not argue amongst ourselves, it won't do us any favours, we're in this together."

"Yes, I suppose," said Mother Nature. "Think of poor Hoppy. He wouldn't have wasted time arguing, would he?"

"When I reaped Hoppy taking him to his cheerful place, why did it look the same as the village, before it burned?"

"We all have a version of heaven, our paradise with the people we love. That was in Hoppy's head, his most cherished place."

"Does that mean my granddad and grandma will have their own little heaven?"

"Yes, I suppose they have somewhere like that."

"Well, if that's the case, who reaped them?"

Father Time shrugged.

"Not sure. Let's move, daylight's fading fast."

They passed a mobile vendor on horseback and stocked up on supplies. Mikey gulped down a pint of Pilichee. At a large stone building with a straw roof he peered in, doubling back when he witnessed a unicorn in a classroom, teaching young magical creatures.

"You can't escape school anywhere!"

"No dear," said Mother Nature "even magical creatures need education!"

A door flew open and out marched the unicorn, livid about the disruption. The students moved to the window and pressed against the glass to peer out.

"Why do you spy into my classroom?"

The unicorn realised Mikey wore the Veil.

"I am in picture perfect health, Mr Reaper. Don't be rash, think of the children, who'll provide education if you reap me?"

"I'm nosing around, apologies for the interruption, this is new to me, I won't reap you."

The unicorn laughed and headed inside, unconvinced.

"That's the first time a teacher feared me."

"Your uncle told me otherwise, didn't you have a run in with a religious education teacher, said you were quite the little terror?"

"It's not my fault I had questions she couldn't answer."

"You ask an awful lot of questions, must run in the family," said Mother Nature.

Angus trotted obediently. It wasn't until Father Time slipped his hand into his pocket and a treat materialised. He knew why.

18.

On the outskirts of a forest, Mother Nature provided information on its origin.

"This forest is supposedly older than time. Last I checked, he'd been around forever!"

"Believe it or not, there are things older than me. We were all kids once; you'd do well to remember that!"

"I can't imagine you young," said Mikey, "you look older than most of these trees here!"

He sniggered and Father Time walked ahead in a huff. The trees in the forest were unlike any he'd ever seen. The bark patterns varied, and each tree had a multitude of colours. Up ahead, Father Time stopped to talk to a group of gnomes who chatted animatedly. He appeared to be the only one in the group who understood them as Mother Nature whispered to Mikey.

"Do you have the faintest idea what they're on about, dear?"

"You're from Majjika, but you don't understand?"

"I started work at three days old dear. I skipped a couple of chapters. Never got to learning Majjikan, if I'm honest. I learned a few choice words, thank you, and another is a swear word!"

It seemed Mother Nature never got a childhood. He didn't press on it but wondered what the swear word was. The gnomes spotted him and backed off. He walked forward to explain he wasn't out to reap them, and they surrounded him, dabbing their little picks into his arms, legs and feet.

"Stop this," said Father Time, "I demand you cease!"

The gnomes walked into the distance, disappearing around a corner. He knelt, removing a shoe. The gnomes drew blood from his now swollen foot. Mother Nature pointed her cane, and he watched in fascination as it healed.

"How can you manage that, but can't fix a tree?"

"A good magician never reveals secrets. Hey, wait, cheeky git!"

She lunged her cane at Mikey. Once she calmed down, he asked.

"What did the gnomes want?"

"They saw a girl headed towards Crummock village and explained we'd need to pass under the mountain. The overpass has been destroyed by those black-eyed kids."

"Fantastic, what's the worst that could happen?"

"Must you moan about everything!"

"Excuse me for not being thrilled about some dark dingy passageway!"

"You moan more than Victor."

"Did my uncle visit Majjika much?"

"At one stage he wasn't away," said Mother Nature, still eyeing Father Time, "I guess when you were there, he'd reason to go home."

"He said this to you?"

"No dear, but he went from one of Father Time's spare bedrooms, to his home again, happier than I'd seen him in a long time."

"He wasn't happy before?"

"No, he missed a part of life most people his age had. You came along and filled that gap."

"I could have helped him, maybe my dad could have?"

"No one other than you and your uncle can know. Eva will too, but we'll cross that bridge later."

"Why did my grandfather hurt Victor? What was he like?"

"Why does anyone hurt, anyone? Charles started out much like you. Rules never applied, he was careless, wanted adventure, nosed around in other people's business and pressed everyone's buttons. When Victor was born, he calmed down a little. When James was born, he seemed to forget all about Majjika."

"He washed his hands?"

"All I know is he didn't listen, like someone else in his family!"

Mikey wondered if he gave the impression he didn't listen. As if she could read his mind, she replied.

"You are here because you didn't listen to your teachers, father and uncle Victor."

"I'm here because my uncle shoved me through that portal!"

"Would he have done so, if you had listened to him about Eva?"

"For the first time in my life I struggled, she helped me settle in."

"Life's a struggle," said Father Time, "but struggles shape who you are today."

"Who am I today?"

"A rule breaker, who won't listen!"

"That's only a part of me?"

"Learn to listen, if not to us, then your inner self."

"I don't understand though. What do you mean?"

"You will in time. For now, we push on."

He followed down a long narrow road that didn't seem to end. No vast mountain in the distance appeared. Angus had his tongue out the side of his mouth. He panted and looked as annoyed as Mikey was. He collided into Father Time, who stopped dead.

"We are here! I see what the gnomes meant. The route above is destroyed, and the mountain by the looks of it!"

He stood beside Father Time, looking to where he pointed. A crumpled wreck of rocks, stones, trees piled up as far as the eye could see.

"We go under the mountain, like the gnomes suggested. The sooner we locate Eva, the sooner I can see Bertha again!"

Mikey muttered the words 'bossy little man' under his breath, audible enough for Mother Nature to hear, and she laughed.

"What's so funny," barked Father Time, "come on, share the joke?"

"Sorry," said Mother Nature, "I erm, laugh when in the face of fear, you know, dark tunnels!"

Angus sniffed the old wooden doors to the underpass entrance. He recoiled in disgust from a foul smell emanating from within. When the doors opened, it took all they had not to vomit.

"What is that awful lingering stench?!"

"That would be stagnant air and water," replied Father Time, "it's obvious they seldom use this pass."

"Surely one of us has some light?"

Father Time pulled out his master watch and whispered into it. It glowed a green colour, then flashed bright yellow,

149

morphing itself into an old-style lantern, like the ones used by miners back in the days before electric. It illuminated the whole tunnel from floor to ceiling.

"That's miles better," said Mother Nature, "avoid those puddles, that's where the stench is!"

"What was the mountain named?"

"It was Crummock mountain to you and me," said Mother Nature, "to the ancestors they knew it as Havvor mountain. Havvor was one of the most respected patron saints of Majjika."

"They had patron saints here, is religion everywhere?"

"We know them as patron saints of Majjika as back when the black-eyed kids first became who they are, they fought to lock them away. Because of that, they were given 'saint' status here. Each had stars, land and even the mountains named after them."

"There have been wars in Majjika?"

"Yes, there have," said Father Time.

"Were they bad?"

"From what I read; some were blood baths."

"Will it happen again?"

"There's potential that should the black-eyed kids gather enough followers, or corrupt people, that war could happen. We should be prepared to stop them. We've done it before; I see no reason we can't lock them back up."

Mother Nature interrupted with a bit of urgency in her voice.

"We must push on, the smell in here is making me rather nauseous!"

19.

Deep into the underpass it became obvious it was the only way around. Creatures passed in the narrow tunnels in the opposite direction. One creature bound by almost bowling them over. They hadn't heard it till the last second. Mother Nature waved her hands in fury.

"Stupid reindeer watch where you trot or expect a hurricane on Christmas day!"

The reindeer scoffed at her and carried on with business. Mikey and Father Time laughed at the expense of Mother Nature.

"Where are we headed?"

Father Time cleared his throat.

"We're headed to Crummock, a very quaint village. I have a minor concern, I forgot to mention the riddles of the nymphs."

"The riddle of what?"

"The riddle of the nymphs. There are four wells. With correct identification of each riddle, you move to the next one. At the end, lies the portal to Earth."

"What happens if you guess incorrectly?"

"To put it bluntly, you remain at the point you failed until someone comes and guesses it right. If you are unlucky, you cease to exist, if you understand what I mean?"

Mikey choked on the bit of biscuit he'd tucked into. It

wasn't as bad as it could've been, Eva could only be a few days ahead, hopefully she had enough food rations. He looked at Mother Nature, who patted him on the back.

"I know what you think. She'll be fine, dear, she's a tough cookie. I'm sure she'll be home already, but if not, we'll get you both back."

"I feel awful. Maybe I should've listened to Victor, then we wouldn't be here. I am to blame, aren't I?"

"To a degree, I suppose. That said, Victor never listened, he did okay. He made one mistake in all the time I've known him. Don't beat yourself up, concentrate on how you can put it right."

Mikey nodded and Mother Nature leant in to hug him. The faint scent of Earth was a welcome smell to the tunnel's putrid stench.

"How long will we be under here?

"I would say we are halfway," said Father Time, "I estimate an hour longer."

They walked in silence when the conversation ran dry. The only one to break the silence was Angus, who sneezed. It echoed around the ravine below. The thunder of water around and below them made it hard to hear anyone.

"Where is that noise from?"

Father Time yelled.

"What!"

"The noise of the water. Where's it from?"

"There is a river below!"

"It's noisy, isn't it!"

"It's quite unique, the water flows upwards, a sight to behold!"

Father Time held his lantern above the handrails, but it

was too dark to see.

The path diverted from the river and the tunnel fell quiet other than the sound of flapping wings. A light flickered; bobbing left to right. Someone approached. Mikey squinted his eyes and tried to figure out who it was. A small creature dressed in what could only be described as a tooth approached, its wings flapped lazily.

"Hello Timothy," said Mother Nature. "How are you?"

He didn't speak but held up his lantern at Mikey. Like everyone else, he froze and tried to blend in with the shadows.

"Hello, Mr Reaper, sir. I wish only to pass by and mean not to disturb you."

"Look, Tim is it, my names Mikey, you need not call me Mr Reaper, okay?"

"Yes, Mikey Sir. I am a tooth fairy who's a little lost at the minute."

"Why you lost, I thought there's only two ways into this tunnel?"

"No, I mean lost on account of not able to get to Earth."

"Why do you need Earth?"

"The teeth. Those poor teeth must be everywhere. What a waste, what a waste!"

He couldn't believe it, first the Easter Bunny and now the tooth fairy, this world was beyond belief.

"So, you exist too?"

"I'm as real as you and the others, sir!"

"It's Mikey."

"Okay, we rarely come across reapers."

"I can say the same for me and tooth fairies. My parents said you weren't real, and they left the money?"

"With all due respect, we don't put money down. We take

the tooth and recycle it, then other children may grow teeth."

"You recycle teeth?"

"We recycle everything."

"So, my parents gave me money! It's fascinating that you recycle baby teeth, I guess they're important."

"Yes, and babies on Earth aren't teething. If this continues, it'll be all over the news. No teeth, no solid food, we'll have a bunch of, excuse me for this, big gummy babies!"

"Ha-ha, that's funny, big gummy babies."

"Your strange for a reaper, didn't think they had a sense of humour. I don't know if I'm surprised or delighted."

"Tim, it's Mikey. How long to the other side?"

"I expect it's twenty minutes. I've a convention to attend, to figure out how we get some teeth."

Father Time addressed Timothy.

"Did you see how the mountain collapsed?

"It was those black-eyed kids. It's a relief to see the back of them, even if they stop us doing our job. How are you coping with manual labour?"

"As well as expected, Timothy. I wish you safe travels, we ought to be on our way. Give my best to your family when you see them, I'm sure you'll be back to stealing teeth in no time."

"We don't steal, we procure and recycle; we borrow them to begin with, they don't grow on trees you know?!"

"Procure, steal, isn't that the same?"

"People would soon complain if we stopped our jobs, that's for sure. We don't steal teeth, I've told you already, they were ours to begin with!"

Mikey rubbed at his teeth. The thought of them in someone else's mouth made him cringe.

"You don't mind humans then? You supply us with teeth

so can't hate us?"

"Humans are greedy. Little kids as young as five want money. It used to be fifty pence, now they want notes and I mean twenty-pound notes, otherwise they scream until the parents give in."

"I've got to admit, kids back home younger than me appreciate nothing!"

"I don't think anyone on Earth does, it's all taken for granted. Those black-eyed kids will have a field day. That said, if they merged the worlds, at least I could get teeth again!"

The tooth fairy shivered, then bid farewell.

When they thought they wouldn't pass anyone else, an odd dreamy looking creature passed. This time the creature wasn't fazed by Mikey.

"Wonderful people, how are we all this bright sunny day."

"We are in a dark tunnel how can you say it's bright," said Mikey, "who are you?"

He took off his hat and bowed.

"It is always bright in Majjika. I'm the reason you have dreams; I can't guarantee the dreams won't turn to nightmares. To answer your question, I am the Sandman. Sandy Sandman at your service."

"Sandy Sandman?"

"Correct, brilliant observation, Michael Birt!"

"How do you know my name?"

"I've dealt with your entire family at one stage, most recently your father. He has had more nightmares this past year, though. He hides many of his feelings away, they manifest themselves when he's asleep."

Mikey felt a small pang of guilt. They were his family, and he hadn't thought about them in days. Sandy placed his hat back on and then put on a pair of sunglasses.

"Bye ladies and gentlemen, I'll see you all soon, even if you don't see me!"

The Sandman disappeared with a whistle. Only his hat and glasses were visible.

"Father Time, who was that?"

"He's a powerful creature, very chilled out, he has to be!"

"Why?"

"If he stressed out, he could alter dreams making them stressful."

"Dreams only exist because of him?"

"Yes and no, it's complicated."

"How can it be yes and no?"

"He tries to help, but there's too many humans on Earth to check every dream."

"The tooth fairy agreed with what the black-eyed kids did, why?"

"Many are displeased with your grandfather. To them he was more human than a magical creature, and not everyone likes humans. They dislike the fact they cause war. I suppose the black-eyed kids offer a different path to follow, corruption is rife. Look at Fredrick Seal."

He had plenty to think about. They walked on but did not pass anyone else, which seemed strange given their interactions with other creatures. Up ahead, Father Time cursed; Earth and boulders blocked their path.

"If I didn't know better, I'd say they wanted us down here. I'll bet they blocked it on both sides. We can't continue onwards, but I fear if we go back, it's the same. What to do, what to do?"

Mother Nature pushed through, waving her walking cane

through the air. The debris moved itself and the dirt moved into piles on the left. The boulders lifted, piling to the right of the tunnel. Angus barked and tried to bite at the Earth as it passed his nose but couldn't get any. Mother Nature sent a pile his way, and he cowered behind Father Time, who looked impressed with the preciseness of Mother Nature's organisational skills. Mother Nature caught sight of Father Time's eyes. She blushed and accidently sent dust towards his face.

"I lost concentration for a second. Please forgive me Father Time."

Father Time wiped his Earth-covered face.

"Can you be more careful, woman; you'll take my eyes out next time!"

Mother Nature nodded. She looked rather abash at how she'd ended what was a superb job.

Mikey broke the tension when he yawned.

"How much further now?"

"I see daylight up ahead and, something else. If I'm not mistaken, it looks like a gate."

Up ahead, a strange-looking creature with a bowler hat sat reading a book. She looked up lazily when they approached.

"Welcome to Crummock village, the toll through the tunnel will be ninety Crystalis per creature."

She looked back at her book, pointing to a collection jar.

"You sat here and didn't notice, less than a hundred metres up, that the path you are charging us for collapsed?"

"Ninety Crystalis per creature," she repeated.

"You would've left us trapped, had it not been for the rather amazing work of Mother Nature!"

"Is that what all that noise was. Keep it down, I'm trying

157

to read my book."

"Are you for real, do you know who I am! I will not pay you one Crystalis to exit this tunnel. One I point out, we fixed for you whilst you sat there. You have the audacity to charge; you didn't even greet us!"

The creature stood to her feet. He hadn't realised how tall she was until she stood up, nor had Father Time by the looks of it. Once again, she pointed to the collection tin. Her eyes glowed a red colour now.

"You pay the fee to go through the gate, or you stay here!"

He grabbed his Crystalis pouch, slamming enough in for the three of them, and walked to the gate, which didn't open.

"You forgot to pay for the dog, that's another ninety Crystalis!"

"You cheeky little, well big. Fine!"

He threw another ninety into the collection jar and the gate vanished so they could pass through to the village.

"I don't know how I didn't projectile vomit. That stench was awful!"

The pass came out near the village. Its houses were quaint, set against what would have been a beautiful mountain. The buildings differed from the village Mikey first landed in all those days ago. This looked like a traditional English village, not a million miles off Croston. The cottages had thatched roofs, and the buildings constructed of white stone. The village square sat to the right and a small inn opposite. Attached to the inn, a black sign with pictures of birds and white writing swung in the breeze. It read 'bird ith hand.'

20.

They rested in the inn overnight. It was the first time Mikey consumed alcohol with permission from adults. Alcohol for teenagers in England involved an elaborate plan to sneak to the local park on a Friday night. Each friend would take it in turns to coerce adults to buy drinks for them from the local booze store. Father Time handed him a handful of Crystalis, leaving him to explore for a while. Seventeen pumps spread across two self-serve bars. You paid the barkeep at the end; she tracked the tabs. The selection on offer ranged from chocolate beer, blackcurrant and liquorice beer, orange beer, Pilichee and violet beer and a fruit salad beer with Pilichee. There were other flavours he didn't dare try like egg and liver beer, Stilton and smoke flavour beer and even a gorgonzola and cocoa beer. Tempted to try the better flavours, he stopped after two when the room spun.

Tired, he joined the others for a few Pilichees. Mikey suffered the aftereffects of the alcohol, but like clockwork, the effects wore off Father Time. When the dawn arrived, they set off and headed out of the village. The sun had come out and the river ice reflected.

Mother Nature walked along. She pointed to various flora and fauna and made the tired ones as good as new. She had also taken to winding Father Time up. A rain cloud had conjured above his head and whenever he looked up it disappeared. On the fifth attempt, he glanced at it.

"It's you! Do you want me to catch the flu? Well, I can't get it, but it's beside the point? These clothes are soaked and I've no change, leave me alone, silly woman!"

Mikey walked ahead to stay out the way as he couldn't help but laugh. A small lake sat ahead of them, and he stopped to admire the view. He removed his shoes and. socks and dipped his feet into the water to cool himself down. He breathed out delighted as the coolness soothed the tiredness of his aching muscles. Angus sniffed the water then turned to walk away from it, changed his mind and bounded into the lake grabbing a stick, which he brought to Mikey and barked like crazy.

"You're supposed to be the guardian of the Veil, not some soft pooch. Oh well, I suppose even you can have fun!"

He threw the stick back into the water and Angus bound after it with a belly flop on the water's surface. The shock waves lapped up against the shore. Mother Nature and Father Time sat down on the lake edge and enjoyed the brief break, the heat and cold water. They'd been there a while when a disturbance behind suggested they had company. Raised voices in the distance grew closer.

"There she is, Mother Nature, we have a situation to square!"

A large congregation of fairies had arrived and seemed furious.

"I think we have a situation; I may have upset them a little, but I can explain, sort of!"

Father Time laughed and said.

"You mean you have a situation."

Mother Nature scowled at a fairy that arrived before the

others. She pointed her wand and shouted. Mikey didn't understand a word she said as it wasn't in English. Mother Nature looked at Father Time and mouthed.

"Help, I don't understand them!"

"Oh fine," said Father Time, "slow down, speak so I may translate!"

The fairy pointed her little wand at Father Time and spoke rather animated.

"I see, I see," replied Father Time, "it seems these fairies had a home in nearby woodland. Someone tried to fix a tree or two and instead burned down half the forest. They spotted a woman with similar if not uncanny looks to Mother Nature. It wasn't you, was it?"

"I erm, I've had difficulties of late trying to get my magic to work, it's like it's all out of whack since the black-eyed kids left and that human girl, Eva arrived."

"See, it wasn't her, wait, don't admit it, they heard what you said, run!!"

The fairies waved their little wands at Mother Nature. She reacted and swatted the closest one to her with her cane, and it flew into a tree. The other fairies growled and flew towards her. Various spells and objects flew towards and around them. They fled as one spell hit Mikey in the face and it swelled up. Father Time sprinted ahead.

"Run already, these little buggers are relentless, Mother Nature jump on my back, we will move faster!"

Mother Nature jumped onto Father Time's back and Mikey howled with laughter. He ran as slow as Mother Nature with her backside held an inch off the floor.

"Come on, faster, faster!"

She yelled for him to run, and his little legs scurried. The angry fairies were relentless and refused to give up the chase for miles. They gained distance on the fairies and took the chance to slip inside an old log cabin. They closed the door and peeked through the blinds at the fairies. The leader of the group pointed.

"They went in that direction, hurry, let's get them!"

Once out of sight, Father Time dropped Mother Nature to the floor.

"Good god, next time you can carry me, what do you keep in your clothes, lead weights?"

"I have heavy bones! If you weren't weak, it wouldn't have been an issue!"

"I am strong enough for my height, thank you very much, when I carried you it proved that!"

"Glad that's over," said Mother Nature, turning away from Father Time.

"That's about more than fire, explain yourself?"

"I may have borrowed from them and never gave back. I was desperate to get my powers back on track. I thought fairy dust could help. It didn't work, and it may have upset them."

Father Time let out a grunt but didn't pursue the conversation. He browsed the photos on the wall, glancing back at one with Victor and other creatures huddled around a campfire. What were the chances of the cabin having pictures of someone they knew?

"Why are my uncle's pictures on the wall?"

Father Time removed the picture from the wall and read from the back panel.

"Victor Birt, Easter Bunny, Timothy Tooth and a few of Santa's little helpers at creatures retreat Majjika, nineteen ninety-two."

"Wow, that was a long time ago. He looked happy there. I wonder what happened to him?"

Father Time grimaced and replied.

"Victor has many problems. He preferred Majjika with non-humans, never seemed to fit in with humankind."

"From the sounds of it, my Dad didn't make it any easier for him. I believe my uncle tried his best, but being a reaper must have taken its toll?"

"Believe me, it did," said Father Time, "he tried his best to balance work and home life, but something had to give. I believe that is why your uncle may have developed a personality disorder, or rather why he ended up stuck in his own head."

"He gave up after my grandfather passed?"

Father Time shifted.

"If it's all right with you, I'd rather not talk about it. I like Victor and I like, should I say, liked Charles."

Father Time avoided eye contact and Mikey put it down to the emotions he felt for his dear friends.

"Victor was a good kid," said Mother Nature. "He always meant well and had everyone's best interests above his own, but sometimes his methods were a little eccentric."

Father Time signalled for her to be quiet, but she carried on regardless.

"Victor was the shadow of his father until the mistake with Eva. He became unconfident, fickle and questionable for his actions."

"What you forget to mention, is the fact that he knew he'd made mistakes and tried to fix them!"

"Made mistakes, that's one way to put it. Those things escaped. I expect you are in denial about Victor, but he did, for all intents and purposes, mess up!

Tired of all the arguments, Mikey turned his attention to Angus, who looked sulky.

"What's up with you? All you worry about is the next meal?"

He covered his face with his paws.

"As much as I love soap operas, do you mind if we go now? We're supposed to be helping each other, not fighting!"

"Sorry," said Mother Nature and Father Time in tandem.

"We're on a time limit to find Eva and you argue like a married couple. That's fine, but I need your help and knowledge right now. Fight later!"

They apologised and headed to the door. Mother Nature noted one photo, tapped Father Time on the back and pointed to it. He walked to the mantle, staring at a photo of Victor and a young woman with blonde hair.

"Ok let's go."

With no mention of the photo, they exited.

21.

Smoke billowed from a chimney in the distance. The ground instantly carpeted in perfect white untouched snow. Mikey rubbed his hands together to keep them warm.

"How can it snow here, but seconds ago it was hotter than July?"

"Well, the weather can vary town by town here. Sometimes you can walk from one boundary across to another and the weather changes. England is like that, is it not?"

"Yeah, England has funny weather. Sometimes it rained and was sunny at the same time. I never quite understood how that worked."

He looked at the tallest peak of the mountains they travelled from a few days ago. These mountains hid the great lake from view.

"Have we come that far?"

"Yes, dear, we travelled from one side of Majjika to the other. Well, we've covered east to west of the major continent. There are small islands around the coast, some protected and others uninhabited. My feet feel the effects now from the distance we walked."

They waited whilst a group of pixies passed them at a crossroads.

"Hello, their Father Time, not used to seeing you on foot?"

"Ah fitness is all the rage now, Nori, you might try it

sometime!"

"No way, that's why we have wings, made for speedy travel!"

Mother Nature looked at Nori, then to a small golden pouch she had strapped around her.

"Nori, I don't suppose you could spare a little pixie dust, I've struggled with magic since the black-eyed kids left."

Nori eyed Mother Nature,

"Sparkle, you have some spare, please share with Mother Nature, we rely on her for the trees we live in!"

Sparkle grabbed her pocket-sized bag and threw it to Mother Nature.

"Thank you very much for this it'll come in handy!"

"Mother Nature," said Nori, "don't use a lot, a pinch is enough."

"Nori, have you seen a human girl?"

"Yes, headed to the wells a few days ago. Good day!"

Nori and the pixies set off in the opposite direction.

"Fantastic news, we aren't too far away!" said Father Time.

Mikey breathed a sigh of relief.

"She wasn't as far up as we thought, I guess she got lost along the way and somehow we caught up. I hope she made it, but if the riddles are like you say, I'm not sure she'll get them all, poor Eva."

"She should be fine with the riddles, dear," said Mother Nature "she seemed bright to me!"

The last village before the wells had a frozen river, leaving a sheet of ice downstream. Mikey watched as they lined up and skated together, little fish-men skated across it. They screamed out in joy. One of them tried to follow her older brother but fell flat on her bottom. She looked up, bawling her eyes out. Like a typical brother, she earned a few harsh words from him about being more careful. She stood up and skulked away. He doubled back when he read the village sign, confused.

"Wait, we've already come from Crummock, haven't we?"

Father Time explained.

"Don't attempt to understand, Majjika. This village is twinned with the other. They're identical in every way."

"What about the residents?"

"I'm glad you asked. This village houses the twins of the other Crummock village. Which was built first? No one knows? Legend says they were constructed the same time, brick by brick. Some say they sprouted up and others believe they've always been here."

"Which arrived first, the chicken or egg?"

Father Time debated this.

"The chicken of course?"

"The egg was around with the dinosaurs. They were around before chickens."

"I suppose, only which came first: the village, or the erm, village?"

Mother Nature chuckled and whispered to Angus.

"Boys will be boys."

Just behind the village stood a stone bridge that stretched over a deep ravine. They got halfway across, and Mikey froze on the spot. Father Time turned back.

"Why did you stop, I know it's high, but man up!"

"It's not that. I can't move, I'm locked to the spot and I feel strange."

Father Time read a sign.

"The Birt's shall not pass this bridge. You're doomed to stay until such a time we let you go. Don't ask why, you know!"

He tried to move his feet, even sneak out of his shoes, but remained stuck to the bridge.

"What do we do, I can't stay here forever? Why punish me for what my family did?"

"I have an idea," said Mother Nature. "It involves a very steady balance; remain still!"

"Erm, what do you have planned?"

"I can release you from the bridge, but it's risky and dangerous if done wrong!"

"What's the alternative?"

"There isn't one. Hold still and I'll free you."

He didn't like the sound of it, but with no alternative, he trusted Mother Nature knew what she was doing. She tapped the bottom of her cane next to his feet and whispered words to it. The ground beneath him shook and the stone boulders beneath him loosened. The mortar in between crumbled, and the stones gave way. He dropped through the bridge with the stone boulders stuck to his feet like lead weights.

"AHHHHH, HELP MEEEEEEE!!"

Mother Nature shrieked and waved her cane. He stopped suspended in mid-air, then glided upwards, back under and around the bridge. Unable to control his descent, the stone boulders loosened themselves and he got up, shaking from head to toe.

"I am so, so sorry. I meant it to be easy, I forgot that cutting away the rock meant you'd tumble. I got it right, eventually!"

He tried to speak, but the five hundred feet near-death

experience left him speechless. He sat at the side of the path and caught his breath.

"Why are they against my family, can I get any further? What else do they have in store?"

"Yes, you can move forwards, don't worry," said Father Time. "The villagers are cautious because when the black-eyed kids were here, they tortured them. That's why they don't like your family, your grandfather is the reason they were shoved in Majjika."

He didn't feel any reassurance as locals peered from their windows. He tried to ignore them, but the last straw was when an elderly elf grabbed a young one by the arm and dragged him inside. Mikey waved away protests and marched over to the door and banged on it. An elf with leathery skin answered.

"What ya want?"

"What have I done to you? I've no control over what my family did!"

"You aren't from round these parts, you aren't welcome, sling ya hook."

"I might not be, but I have emotions you know!"

The elf ignored him.

"Where is he?"

"Who are you on about?"

The elf spat his words.

"Victor of course, where is he?"

"Why do you care where my uncle is?"

"He'd be dead if any of us had our way, useless, absolutely useless!"

Mikey lunged for the elf.

"That's my uncle, you short little git. What did he do to you? You'll wish you were dead for that!"

He struggled against Mikey's grip, choking.

"Took folk away from this village, young ones who never got to live their lives, don't you dare talk to me about him!"

"It was his job; he didn't have a choice. Do you think we take pleasure in it? We do it because we have to!"

"When it's your son or daughter taken; you might not take lightly to it. Explain all you like, but a child should never pass before their parents. It's not right!"

The elf fell into tears and ran inside with a slam of the door. Mikey never thought about it before. The elf had a point. No parent should bury their child. They walked in silence, and it was a while before Father Time broke it outside a dingy shop.

"We should buy supplies in case we're stuck in the tunnels with the riddles."

They crowded into a small, dimly lit shop with barely any natural light. A green coloured man emerged from the back, standing behind the counter. He scowled at Mikey, then greeted Father Time like an old friend.

"If it's not Time himself, how are you, old chap?"

"Good afternoon Sully, I hope all's well? I wish to purchase food rations and some Pilichee. We're headed to the wells. Better to prepare!"

"Your off to the wells, with this one here," said Sully concerned, "best be careful, slippery folk these reapers, no disrespect meant of course!"

Mikey growled and Mother Nature stood on his foot and held her arm out.

"Don't rise to it, calm down it's not worth it, believe me."

"If you're going into the wells, you must be headed to Earth. I don't get why you do it manually, Father Time, can't you zap yourself there?"

"Yes, normally I could Sully. It seems those creatures stopped us somehow. It has been strenuous, manual labour!"

Mikey and Father Time had a very different view on what manual labour was, but he kept his thoughts to himself and allowed the conversation to continue.

"I hear the riddles have become extra difficult since those things escaped. Not sure if they keep us in, or them out!"

Father Time shot a worried look for a second at Mother Nature.

"I'm sure we will figure them out, there's three of us. May I ask a question?"

Sully ducked and pulled up Pilichee from under his counter, stacking them against each other.

"What question would that be?"

"Have you spotted a young girl, brown hair, brown eyes," answered Father Time, "taller than me, she goes by the name Eva Lyfer?"

"That wouldn't be hard, you're three feet tall on a good day!"

Father Time shot a filthy look at Sully, who backtracked and answered the question.

"She shouldn't be in Majjika, that girl's more confused than a troll with a Rubik's cube!"

"That's what I feared," said Father Time, "thank you for the information Sully, how much do I owe you for the supplies?"

Sully looked at Mikey, contemplated charging more, but thought better of it.

"That'll be two-hundred and twenty Crystalis, please."

Father Time paid, then they departed towards the wells.

22.

The entrance to the caves leading to the wells glimmered in the light. Its support pillars, made of diamond, were remarkable. The light hit them, but instead of it being reflected, they absorbed it; they glowed beautifully. The light travelled from one pillar to the other, when someone walked by. They stopped in the main cavern to take in its magnificence. A waterfall cascaded into a gully below, filling the air and reflecting light from the cave. Stalactites and stalagmites lined the roof and floors. Mikey picked up that the cave didn't echo in the slightest.

"What's special about nymphs, how are they powerful enough to guard these portals?"

Father Time touched and observed the diamond pillars.

"The simple answer is nymphs are impervious to magic. They're not affected by corruption or deception; it's why the black-eyed kids couldn't get out. They remained trapped on Majjika, powerless. That was until your uncle upset the balance and allowed them to escape. They have an ancient protection that no one can break, unless you answer the riddles designed by each nymph. They change each time you pass, so use of these portals is risky."

"Why the wells, aren't they too small for portals?"

"The wells contain a liquid which links to Earth. It looks like water, acts like water, but is so much more. It's complicated to explain, but they bind the two places together. We used to have different, larger gates but the erm, guardians decided they wanted to do other things.

Mikey willed Father Time to carry on.

"There used to be another way?"

"There used to be main gates we could come and go as we pleased. The witch hunts happened on Earth, and magical creatures of all kinds found themselves in the middle of a war zone. The high council of Majjika deemed it unsafe for all to travel, unless in an emergency. They opened smaller portals up to drip feed creatures in and out. That made us less likely to be spotted by humans on Earth. Humans still catch sight of us. Father Christmas has been in front of the council three dozen times for being seen."

"The Salem witch trials, and the Lancashire witch trials affected Majjika?"

"We took precautions and no magical creatures as far as I am aware were hurt. We adapted, and creatures became more cautious in the human world. The main gates remained closed, then the smaller portals opened."

"Why didn't the gates reopen?"

"It was easier for the council to monitor, only the privileged leave Majjika."

Mikey sniffed a faint aroma of perfume. The delightful fragrance meandered its way through the caves from the bottom of some marble steps.

"I'm guessing it's that way down the stairs?"

Mother Nature answered.

"Yes, it's down that way. I don't want to hold your hand but be careful. That perfume you can smell, it's enticing. If you're not careful, they will ensnare you!"

Mother Nature lifted her foot up in the air and kicked Angus, who was lay asleep on the ground. He groaned and stood up.

"Well come on let's go, we are close to Eva, I feel it."

Mikey wondered if Mother Nature could sense Eva's presence in the tunnels ahead, or if she meant they were close to Mikey and Angus leaving her in peace.

The faint aroma of the perfume became ever more prominent. Mikey felt at ease with each breath until he didn't care about anything. He was surprised and had to recompose himself when Mother Nature asked a personal question. Whatever affected him, she was immune too.

"You don't speak to your father at all now?"

"I don't, I haven't spoken to either parent since I got to my uncle's. My relationship with them wasn't good, it seems they never even checked to see I arrived."

"Family is a funny thing dear, you can't pick them, sometimes you wish you could!"

"You have a family?"

"A long time ago, I had family. We all came from somewhere. Only my upbringing was, well, a quick one. My mother fell ill, and I had to take over the family business. The reason I have this bonsai tree on my hat is because it belonged to my mother, it was the first thing she ever grew I couldn't leave it behind,"

Tears streamed down her face and she wiped them.

"That's in the past, we must move in the present, never backwards!"

Ahead, Angus barked at someone. A smooth voice filled the air, and he became quiet instantly. Up ahead, the figure of a creature came into view. She was the most beautiful creature

Mikey had ever seen, and she wore a white dress, her long strawberry blonde hair waved from side to side. Her perfect skin glowed in the light.

"Good dog, there's a beautiful boy, lie down now. Relax, you can stay here as long as you want."

They approached her and she looked around until she noticed Mikey. She floated over to him and looked into his eyes. His heartbeat with such force he was sure it echoed through him.

"Well, hello there. Two humans in the same week! I like you better, you are very handsome,"

Mikey gulped, trying to speak, but glowed red in the face, looking at his shoes. The nymph giggled, and Father Time mimicked this, who seemed affected by the nymph.

"Oh, Father Time, you look as cute as ever!"

Father Time puffed up his chest and smiled. Behind the nymph about twenty feet away, a well glowed blue. She noticed Mikey's eyes dart towards it and moved to block it.

"I see you have the Veil of the reaper. Such a burden that must be. Why not stay here with me?"

He nodded and sat on the floor, mesmerised. Mother Nature cleared her throat when no one responded. She rapped Mikey on the head with her cane and he jumped up.

"What did I tell you, don't get distracted! It's all a trick to keep you from the wells. Concentrate on more than the superficial beauty of this harlot!"

The nymph looked through Mother Nature and turned her attention to Father Time again.

"What about you, my big, muscular man? You want to stay here forever and keep me company, don't you?"

Father Time giggled, his cheeks turned red, and then his

eyes glazed over.

"She's mine, I will stay here and protect my love. You will leave us. She's mine. Go away, you had your chance!"

Mikey rubbed at his sore head and grabbed Father Time around the waist. He pulled him off the ground and lifted him into the air and carried him forwards. Father Time punched and kicked out; Mikey dropped him to the ground with a thud. Father Time looked up at them, confused.

"What happened? Ooh, you, you tried to entice me! Let us through!"

The nymph threw her hair behind her shoulders and her demeanour changed.

"You won't stay with me, very well! You guess the riddle you can move forwards, guess it wrong and I'll shut you in here forever!"

Mikey pushed past to the first well.

"What do we do, how do we move to the next one?"

The nymph replied.

"All step into the wishing well, the liquid will lock you in. Guess my riddle right and I'll allow you to progress, guess it wrong and you'll leave the well and you're stuck here, until someone guesses the riddle right. That's if I don't keep you all as my little pets!"

"You've kept us long enough, give us the riddle will you so we can get to Eva!"

"That Lyfer girl is your friend, how ironic, ha-ha!"

"What do you mean, ironic?"

"Oh, never mind, here is my riddle. I won't repeat, so listen!"

"You might find me with a bed or a shore, I can be liquid, gas or solid, I run but don't have legs, and I often reflect, what

176

am I?"

Mikey thought it sounded simple, but under pressure and with her watching, it made it hard to work out what it could be.

"What is she on about?"

Mother Nature didn't reply. Mikey turned to Father Time to ask if he knew when Mother Nature clapped her hands excitedly. She bobbed up and down on the balls of her feet and shouted.

"It's water!"

"Are you sure it's water, Father Time, what do you think it is?"

"I think it's water, but what if it's water, like the ocean, a lake, a river?"

Mikey put his head in his hands.

"If we guess the wrong answer, is that it. No second guesses, no more chances?"

"You each get one guess. Make your guesses when you're ready but be quick, I'm bored!"

Father Time blurted,

"Is it a river?"

The nymph smiled and nodded, then cackled.

"Nope, one guess down, two to go ha-ha!"

Mother Nature hesitated. Through her hands, she asked.

"Is it the ocean?"

"Nope, one guess left, come on human, answer the riddle?"

"My guess for the riddle would be a lake, maybe?"

"Ooh, too bad. All three guesses were wrong, looks like you're here with me after all!"

Mikey thought quickly.

"Technically, there's four of us. Does that mean we get four guesses?"

The nymph growled.

"You cheeky human, I, well, very well, I'll give you one last guess!"

Mother Nature interjected.

"It's water, the definitive answer, water!"

The nymph signalled to the liquid underneath their feet, which bound itself to them and made its way upwards. The cold crept up as the liquid surrounded them. Before it reached Father Time's mouth, she said.

"Best hold your breath, this could well kill you, ha-ha!"

Father Time held his breath as the liquid covered him, Angus did the same thing and then Mother Nature and Mikey were engulfed by the liquid. The ground beneath gave way. They cascaded down a narrow tunnel and bounced them from side to side. Slithers of light lit the tunnel walls. It felt like it went on forever. Mikey about ready to lose consciousness panicked when he swallowed the liquid. He gasped for air and was about to pass out when they were ejected. He coughed up liquid, which crawled its way back into the pool behind them. Mikey caught his breath and looked around. The tunnel was bigger, with hand carved yellow and green rock.

Yet another nymph approached. This time she had brown hair and pink lips.

"I see you beat my sister's first riddle and resisted her charms, well done. You won't be so lucky with me!"

Mikey looked at the nymph. She dressed in tree branches and leaves that covered her body. He approached, and she broke into speech.

"To pass, you must…

"We already know, we have to answer the riddle! Give it us, will you?"

The nymph broke into chorus.

"I am strong, but I am weak, I can whistle with no mouth, and move trees with ease. I howl if I'm strong, or I quietly move along. What am I?"

"Did you say howl if I'm strong?"

The nymph nodded.

"I don't know if they exist, but on a whim, I'd say, werewolf?"

The nymph heckled Mikey.

"A werewolf? Wrong answer!"

"Could you be so kind, as to repeat the riddle?"

The nymph obliged Father Time.

"I am strong, but I am weak, I can whistle with no mouth, and move trees with ease. I howl if I'm strong, or I quietly move along. What am I?"

"I want to say a bear, is it a bear?"

"Not a bear. Not clever, are you Father Time?"

"If you were any other creature, I'd have punished you for that remark. As I can't do anything, I'll settle with this, you're not half as attractive as your sister!"

The nymph diverted her attention to Mother Nature.

"It seems its left to the female of the group. Seeing as you're oldest, you'll be the wisest!"

"Looks fade dearie, you might be pretty now, but that'll fade. You'll be an empty husk with an ugly personality. The answer is wind!"

The nymph shrieked and her body combusted into flames.

"You, horrible old hag, fine, go, leave me alone!"

Inside the next well, they felt a breeze overhead. The

breeze turned to wind and held them down on the spot. The well opened, and they dropped into a large pit. Inches off the ground, the wind picked up and stopped them hitting the floor. Mikey adjusted himself, landing on his feet. Mother Nature and Father Time landed in a heap as Angus landed gracefully, he'd had a lot of practice with portals.

The third nymph didn't even bother with an introduction.

"I keep you warm, and help you see, when all else fails, you'll need me. I help you cook; I'll help you clean, but if used wrong, I can be mean. What am I?

Father Time replied straight away.

"Fire, of course."

The nymph moved away from the well she protected, looking disappointed. They climbed in. An immense heat crossed over them, the flames engulfed either side.

"Stay still, wouldn't want any of you crispy now!"

The flames span and danced around. Mikey couldn't open his eyes or breathe. A noise like a breaking tree bow filled the air and the floor underneath opened, sending them into a chute. The heat made the walls hot around them. He covered his skin to stop the burning. Angus yelped in pain and Mikey grabbed him, holding him off the floor. At the bottom, they landed in a pile.

23.

A light flickered from side to side. Mikey was certain he heard an angry voice echo down the tunnel. The light flickered again, accompanied by the unmistakable voice of Eva Lyfer. He cried with relief, the guilt he felt lifted away from him. He called out, and she looked around with her lamp. She spotted them and stormed over, slapping Mikey. Tears covered her face.

"Is that you?"

"It's me. It took goodness knows how many days to track you down, I'm sorry about my unc…"

She slapped him several times.

"Do you know how hard it's been for me. I don't understand what's happened, I'm stuck in some, some world full of Magical creatures, and your uncle is one of them!"

"I didn't know, I've searched for you everywhere, trust me. I travelled to the edge of Majjika and back to find you, I'm sorry!"

"Sorry?! You think an apology will fix this. What must my mum think, she'll be worried sick? Do you realise the effort it took to get to this riddle? I couldn't guess it. Now I'm stuck here forever, unable to go back, unable to move forward!"

"No, Eva, you're not stuck. If we guess the riddle, we all get to go home. It's complicated. Earth needs help. The black-eyed kids escaped and are on Earth, Victor's in trouble and we're the only ones who can help!"

"Good, I'm glad he's in trouble. I could have died here! You can get me home, as soon as we're there, I want nothing to do with you or your stupid uncle ever again, I hate you!"

She walked to the corner of the cave and sat down with her back towards Mikey on a makeshift bed. He looked at Father Time and Mother Nature. Hurt by the sudden hatred, he walked over to sit next to her and placed his arm over her shoulder. When she didn't move, he spoke.

"I didn't know where you'd gone. I had the police asking me questions on your whereabouts, my uncle lied through his teeth about it. I got shoved through a portal into another world, which confused me. I wanted to find you, I wanted to get you home! I miss my friend, you're the first person I can be myself around.

"I've been here God knows how long and that's the best you have, I mean, where are we?"

"We're in some cave, the wells of Nymphoria in Majjika."

"No, I mean, where are we, as in me and you?"

He looked into Eva's eyes and wiped the tears from underneath.

"I liked you the moment I saw you, now isn't the time to discuss it. We need to get out of here. I'll explain later, I promise!"

Eva wanted to ask another question, but Father Time barked.

"Hate to break up the reunion, we must get you back to Earth, you must rescue Victor from those damn evil beings."

"The two of you wouldn't help me no matter how much I begged, but you helped Mikey. That's fantastic!"

Father Time shuffled around, and Mother Nature looked away, ashamed.

"I've been here that long I can't remember what day it is; we can't go until one of us solves the final riddle!"

Eva kicked stones towards the last nymph who crept up behind them whilst distracted. The well was bigger than the others, with strange words glowing on its walls. Steps led up to the semi suspended liquid. Mikey cleared his throat.

"Give me the riddle, I want to go home!"

The nymph sang a glass shatteringly shrill song, and it took self-control not to block his ears.

"I am the present, I am the past, but in the future, I will not last. When you're almost nearly there, I'll disappear without a care. What am I?"

Mikey glanced at Eva, who raised her eyebrows.

"If I guessed the answer, I wouldn't be here, would I?"

Mikey opened his mouth to retaliate but resisted. Father Time repeated the words over pacing the tunnel.

"I'll disappear without a care well, I think I know the answer, but would anyone care to guess first?"

Mikey thought about it.

"Is it my parents?"

Father Time shouted out.

"Don't be stupid boy, why would it be your parents!"

The nymph laughed.

"Aw poor boy you, no love from his parents and is bitter. Nope wrong answer, two guesses left then you are all here with me!"

Mother Nature scrunched her nose and blurted.

"Is it air, you can never grab air, but it's always there?"

The nymph broke into dance again.

"Wise choice air, but not the right answer. Looks like it's all down to you, old man!"

183

Father Time infuriated with the old man comment yelled.

"You'll regret that. I'll get the answer, I need a minute to think."

The nymph smirked.

"Take all the time you need, I'm here forever."

Father Time continued to pace and pulled out his pocket watch, flicked the glass case open and closed it.

"The answer, is time, isn't it? Time, that is my final answer!"

The nymph clapped, sarcastically.

"Father Time, guesses after what seems like forever, the one thing he's in charge of!"

"It's not the length of the journey it's the result that counts. Now open that damn portal so we can be on our way, nymph!"

The nymph stepped aside, and the portal erupted into life.

"How did you guess that? I've been here for days. You listen once and guess the answer."

"Hello, I am Father Time. If I couldn't figure out that one, assume the universe would be screwed."

Mikey couldn't help but laugh. Eva laughed a little too. They walked up into the well, but Mother Nature hadn't followed.

"You're not coming with us, are you?"

"No dearie, I have to go back to my day job. It's been an adventure. Best of luck, I'm sure I'll see you in the future."

"Thanks for the help. I couldn't have got here if it weren't for you."

Father Time didn't speak and seemed to contemplate something. He looked like someone who carried the world on his shoulders.

"Eva, I know you are mad, but please understand Victor does silly things when he's under pressure. He wouldn't have meant to do what he did. Please help him find his uncle and get him home."

"Not sure how I feel, I've got lots to think about. I want to go home and hug my mum. Why can't you help Mikey find his uncle, you helped him here?"

"I suppose, but I've lots to do and if I let it go wayward, the consequences could be disastrous!"

Father Time shifted, and Mikey understood what was wrong.

"You, you're terrified of them, aren't you, the black-eyed kids?"

"No, not at all I dislike them. They, they don't scare me!"

Father Time looked to the floor and didn't meet his gaze.

"If you're terrified, face your fears head on!"

"Look, even if I wanted to, there's too, fine, I'll help you!"

"Mother Nature, it has been a pleasure. You have been brilliant company. I hope we can be together again soon; I mean see each other, again, bye!"

Mother Nature smiled at the group and bid her farewell. She tapped her cane against the ground and disappeared.

Mikey yelled out.

"Wait, how did she do that?!"

The nymph, still stood close by, responded.

"As you guessed the riddles, you can return to Majjika or through the portal to Earth. She chose Majjika."

"I guess for now this is it for us. Do we go through the portal together?"

"Let's all go together, step in and I'll follow behind.

Mikey held Eva's hand to help her up over the edge of the

steps and they stepped into the portal. It kicked into life but before it could carry them away Father Time glimpsed someone familiar and walked backwards. For a second, he swore he saw his mother, someone who'd passed many years ago. The portal span upwards and they disappeared. Father Time stood on his own. He looked to the corner where he thought he'd seen his mother. From behind, a confident, devious voice spoke.

"Hello Brother!"

Father Time turned, grabbed his pocket watch and vanished.

24.

They tumbled in near darkness and he called out, making sure she was okay. A few retching noises later, she responded.

"Err, yeah, I'm okay, bit nauseous. How long will this take!?"

"Last time it seemed like forever. Where's Angus, I swear he was here a second ago? The Veil, it's gone!"

He felt in the dark for it. It was on when he entered the portal.

The portal shot open, and they catapulted to the floor.

"Ouch!"

He helped Eva to her feet and looked around the dark room they landed in. Something wasn't right. He walked forward with his hands out and panicked when he touched iron bars and a thick lock. Eva stood to the side of him, feeling the bars.

"Is this another riddle to solve?"

He searched but still couldn't find him. Angus followed the Veil but was nowhere to be seen.

"Are you even listening to me?"

When he didn't reply she shouted.

"What are you looking for! I am pretty certain you won't find it; you've covered the floor fifty times!"

"It's hard to explain, it's a Veil that sits over my clothes.

"That creepy thing that you had on, I assumed it English

fashion, although your uncle wore one like it!"

"You could see it all along. I don't understand, why did you never mention it? Didn't it seem strange to you?"

"When he threw me from your house, I forgot about it. The second time I visited, well we ended up here didn't we."

"I can't find it, it's too dark to look. I doubt it's here."

Why could she see the Veil, but he couldn't until passed to him? It made little sense. Certain there was more, had she made Angus disappear to spite Victor?

"If you see the Veil, you know more than you're saying. I know you're mad at me and my uncle, but please don't take it out on Angus. He's the guardian, he protects and watches over the keeper."

"As angry as I am, what would I do with a dog twice my weight in the short time we've been together, you've seen my every move. What's special about the Veil, and why is Angus different? I mean, I sense it's the same dog, only different?"

"It's complicated to explain. We're reapers, taking people to the other side. If the Veil's lost, no one can move on."

It occurred to him how messed up this seemed. He had a blessing, or rather a curse no one knew about. Lost in his own head, he'd drowned out Eva and zoned back in when she shook his shoulder.

"If the Veil is important and these black-eyed kids are dangerous, and now we're stuck, does it mean it's a trap?"

"Not sure, but it's gone. I'd say it's bad."

"I'd say more than bad. Look."

A light appeared, and a door opened. The cabin lit dimly to reveal Angus and one creature he'd dreaded seeing again.

A small child white as a ghost with black eyes smiled maliciously.

"Who the hell are you," Eva barked, "why take Angus!?"

"What are the chances we'd meet. You have something we want, trade it for, say, your life?"

"I have what you want? What happened to your eyes they're black? Mikey, why are you afraid of these kids?"

"Don't you dare talk to me like that! We are far more powerful than you. Stop the stall tactics and give us what we want, or we will find it anyway and leave you here with this, reaper to rot."

"I have nothing you want, you said we, but I only see you, give him back already!"

"Funny thing about this dog, he's linked to the Veil. No deal!"

"That belongs to my family, give it back!"

"The brave reaper speaks up, I wondered if you were letting your girlfriend do the talking!"

He grabbed the iron bars between them.

"Let me out, and we'll see who protects who!"

"Why would I do that? Why don't you ask your girlfriend where the golden headband is? There's a good boy, ha-ha!"

"What's he on about, a golden headband?"

"I don't know, I swear!"

"Hey, come here boy, please."

Angus didn't move.

"He won't listen. He listens to the keeper, oh that would be me!"

"Who are you?"

"I am a god. I have a name; in your tongue it is Arce Porter. That maybe the last name you hear. Enough chit chat, it's obvious you won't help, stay here and rot!"

Yet more vile creatures piled in. They spoke to each other

in hushed voices, only the odd cackle audible.

Arce spoke, and they fell silent.

"We cannot afford to fail brothers and sisters, we must find the golden headband and the other artefacts, it's crucial for our survival, our master plan!"

They cheered, and the sound sent a chill through his spine.

"What have you done with my uncle, you better not hurt him or else I'll…"

"You're in no position to make threats. Trapped behind a cell door with no key, you won't escape. Not like the escape from Fredrik Seal's dungeon!"

"Wait, that was you?!"

"We have many friends. How do you think we plotted our escape! Enough! We carry on with our plan. We must succeed! As for your uncle, we have plans for him. For now, he's alive. Goodbye Michael Birt, Eva Lyfer, it's been a pleasure!"

The one closest to the door pulled it open, and they piled out. The door slammed shut and Mikey slumped to the floor, burying his head in his hands. They were trapped, no Angus, no Veil or way of escaping. He glanced up when he felt a soft hand on his shoulder.

"We'll find a way out, don't worry. Something always comes from nothing."

"Don't worry! You don't understand, they have the Veil. It wasn't some stupid creepy thing on my head. It served a purpose. Now they are stronger than ever, Victor's gone, and we're trapped.

"We have to get it back then, don't we? There must be a way to escape. This iron door looks normal to me, no magic about it, I don't think!"

"How can you accept there's magic? How can you be

relaxed?"

"I can't explain, but we'll be okay. Thanks for coming to get me. At least if I'm stuck somewhere, I'm not alone."

"I don't understand. Victor sent me to Majjika to find you. He said he'd made a mistake and you're more important than he realised."

"That's odd. I'm plain old Eva."

Sitting in silence, Mikey found it hard not to sob. In a rage, he jumped against the door, kicking it hard. He tried to ram it with his shoulder and borrowed a hair pin to pick the lock. Both exhausted, they collapsed in anguish. Mikey drifted between sleep and it wasn't until a bright light filled the room that he regained consciousness. The light hovered above their heads, searching. It passed through the door.

"Did you see that light?"

"Yeah, I saw it, but I don't understand, it looked like…"

Before she finished, the door in front blasted into pieces, blown clean off its hinges.

The brightest light filled the doorway with the outline of a woman.

Mikey covered his eyes.

"Mother Nature is that you. Help, we're both stuck in here!"

The light softened and in walked one of the most beautiful women he laid eyes on.

"Mother Nature, I'm not half as kind!"

The accent of the woman sounded familiar and his suspicions were confirmed.

"Mum is that you, it's actually you, oh my God. How did you find me? Be careful there's some creature out there, it's hard to explain!"

"I should have used my better judgement, another Birt. How could that not have gone wrong! Your family has been trouble for me. I suppose this was Victor's idea, thinking he can stop you two being together?"

"He sent me, wait, you know Victor? How did you find me?"

"That's my uncle you're talking about. Be careful what you say!"

"Don't make me laugh. Your uncle is a reckless fool who thinks the laws of Majjika don't apply."

"Mum, how do you know about Majjika?"

"I've been meaning to tell you. It's complicated to explain. We are a part of the same coin, different sides, but the same coin. There's more than Victor, who knows about Majjika. Stay back, I need to break you out!"

She stepped back and pointed to the iron bars which heated glowing bright red. Eva looked terrified.

"Mum, there's a key to your left, use the key!"

"Yeah, that would be easier!"

She placed the key in the lock and opened the door.

"Mum, what are those kids on about? The golden headband. Wait, I see it on your head. I thought you said that's a trinket from grandma, a hand-me-down!"

"We are Lyfers. Think of you and Mikey as ying and yang, you do the jobs together, so we have equilibrium. His family reaps souls that need to move on to their resting place. We save the ones whose time hasn't come. We've done this for millennia. Our families haven't always seen eye to eye, and the Birt's are the ones who made it difficult, of course!"

She paused for a moment.

"If we are to rescue your uncle, who I'm assuming is in

trouble, you're going to need to learn how to use the Veil properly. Where is the it?"

"Well, the thing about that is."

"You bloody idiot, please don't tell me they have it?"

Mikey nodded.

"Victor's reckless, although he didn't lose the Veil after five minutes. This is a disaster. Where is he?"

She peered into his eyes and an uneasy sensation spread through the pit of his stomach.

"They got him, took him away. He sent me to get Eva and saved my life. Those things are evil!"

Ava confused for a minute.

"Wait, they are here, on Earth?!"

She pinned him against the wall.

"They're here on Earth and you let them walk without informing the council of Majjika? Do you realise what you and your family have done!"

"I, didn't, know," said Mikey gasping for air, "I'm new, to this!"

"Mum let him go, you'll kill him! Mum!"

"A Lyfer killing a reaper, the irony," said Ava, "they are in this world, which means they'll search for artefacts. Combined, they do one of two things. Lock those kids away or bind worlds to control everything!"

"They'll control everything if they get the artefacts?"

"Yes, and we'll be powerless, unless we act fast. Of course, we are slowed because you misplaced the Veil!"

"Not misplaced, stolen. We were with Father Time; he didn't come through the portal?"

"That's worrying, I hope they didn't capture him. Eva, you look exhausted, come here."

She pulled her into a hug and burst into tears.

Mikey felt an incredible amount of guilt flow through him. But they couldn't stay here.

"I'm sorry to break up the hug, I think we should leave, before they return. I don't fancy lingering!"

They followed Ava's light, which hovered through the air.

"What now, Eva's mum?"

"It's Ava, Ava Lyfer."

"What now?"

"It's simple. We rescue your idiot uncle!"